BACH PERSPECTIVES

VOLUME SEVEN

J. S. Bach's Concerted Ensemble Music,
The Concerto

BACH PERSPECTIVES

VOLUME SEVEN

Editorial Board

George B. Stauffer, General Editor, Mason Gross School of the Arts, Rutgers University

Bach
Perspectives

VOLUME SEVEN

J. S. Bach's Concerted Ensemble Music,
The Concerto

Edited by Gregory Butler

UNIVERSITY OF ILLINOIS PRESS · URBANA AND CHICAGO

ISSN 1072-1924
ISBN-10 0-252-03165-2
ISBN-13 978-0-252-03165-6

Bach Perspectives is
sponsored by the
American Bach Society
and produced under the
guidance of its Editorial
Board. For information
about the American Bach
Society, please see its
Web site at this URL:
www.americanbachsociety.org.

CONTENTS

PREFACE

Volumes 6 and 7 of *Bach Perspectives*, devoted to the concerted ensemble music of J. S. Bach, are most timely. In recent years there has been a surge of interest on the part of Bach scholars, particularly in the composer's concertos, the subject of the present volume. This interest was greatly stimulated by the first Dortmünder Bach-Symposion in 1996 devoted to Bach's orchestral works and the publication of the proceedings from this conference the following year. The Bach year in 2000 saw the publication of a comprehensive study of the concertos, Siegbert Rampe and Dominik Sackmann's *Bachs Orchesterwerke*, which has provoked considerable reaction in the world of Bach scholarship.

The Bach Colloquium at Harvard University has been an important forum for lively discussion of various issues surrounding these works, and two of the essays in this volume, those by Gregory Butler and David Schulenberg, were first presented in early stages of preparation before this group and now appear in print. As such, these two volumes, 6 and 7, add a primarily American voice to the ongoing scholarly discourse centering on this group of works of such importance for Bach studies.

Gregory Butler, President
The American Bach Society

EDITOR'S PREFACE

This volume of *Bach Perspectives*, along with its sister volume already published as *Bach Perspectives* 6, marks the extension of a project begun with my early collaboration on volume 4 of the series, edited by David Schulenberg and published in 1999. The intention to bring out a collection of essays devoted entirely to Bach's concerted ensemble music, only partly realized in two studies by Jeanne Swack and myself in the earlier volume, has now come to fruition in volumes 6 and 7. The first of these focuses on the ouverture, a genre of concerted ensemble music that has received remarkably little attention in the scholarly literature of late, and the second centers on the concertos of Bach, an area that has attracted considerable scholarly attention and debate.

The opening two essays in the present volume are a study in contrasts, in that they come to diametrically opposed conclusions concerning the origins of two of the concertos for solo cembalo, for which the original versions do not survive. In the opening essay, I call on evidence provided by the sources for the E-Major Concerto (BWV 1053)—in particular, the correction of transposition errors—to demonstrate that Bach resorted to the expedient of *bricolage*, the assembling of concertos by recycling preexistent isolated concerted movements with different origins. In the following study, Pieter Dirksen, in focusing on the early source history of the F-Minor Concerto (BWV 1056), presents important source evidence and analyses in support of his view that the work's origins lie in a G-minor violin concerto.

The third essay, by David Schulenberg, offers new perspectives on what has been a major issue of Bach studies, the *auf Concertenart* sonata. In doing so, it raises more fundamental questions concerning how Bach conceived of the concerto early in his career and how that concept evolved over time.

Finally, Christoph Wolff's study focuses on the *siciliano*, establishing it as an important subgenre for slow concerto movements of Leipzig provenance. His essay goes on to explore the implications of the late chronology of a specific siciliano, BWV 1053/2, for the concerto's performance history and the identity of its solo instrument.

Gregory Butler
Vancouver, British Columbia

ix

ABBREVIATIONS

BDOK   Werner Neumann and Hans-Joachim Schulze, eds. *Bach-Dokumente.* 4 vols. Kassel: Bärenreiter; Leipzig: VEB Deutsche Verlag für Musik, 1963–78.

BG   [Bach-Gesamtausgabe.] Johann Sebastian Bach's Werke. Edited by the Bachgesellschaft. 47 vols. Leipzig: Breitkopf & Härtel, 1851–99.

BJ   *Bach-Jahrbuch.*

BWV   [Bach-Werke-Verzeichnis.] Wolfgang Schmieder, ed. *Thematisch-systematisches Verzeichnis der musikalischen Werke von Johann Sebastian Bach.* Rev. ed. Wiesbaden: Breitkopf & Härtel, 1990.

BOM   Siegbert Rampe and Dominik Sackmann. *Bachs Orchestermusik: Entstehung, Klangwelt, Interpretation.* Kassel: Bärenreiter, 2000.

BOW   Martin Geck and Werner Breig, eds. *Bachs Orchesterwerke.* Dortmunder Bach-Forschungen 1. Witten: Klangfarben-Verlag, 1997.

HWV   [Händel-Werke-Verzeichnis] Bernd Baselt, *Verzeichnis der Werke Georg Friedrich Händels*, in *Händel-Handbuch*, 4 vols. Kassel: Bärenreiter, 1978.

KB   Kritischer Bericht (critical report) of the NBA.

KBT   Ulrich Siegele, *Kompositionsweise und Bearbeitungstechnik in der Instrumentalmusik Johann Sebastian Bachs*, Tübinger Beiträge zur Musikwissenschaft 3, ed. Georg von Dadelsen. Neuhausen Stuttgart: Hänssler-Verlag, 1975.

NBA   [Neue-Bach-Ausgabe.] *Johann Sebastian Bach: Neue Ausgabe sämtlicher Werke.* Edited by the Johann-Sebastian-Bach-Institut, Göttingen, and the Bach-Archiv, Leipzig. Kassel: Bärenreiter; Leipzig: Deutscher Verlag für Musik, 1954–.

NBR   Hans T. David and Arthur Mendel, eds. *The New Bach Reader: A Life of Johann Sebastian Bach in Letters and Documents.* Revised and enlarged by Christoph Wolff. New York: W. W. Norton & Co., 1998.

P   Berlin, Staatsbibliothek zu Berlin, Mus. ms. Bach Partitur (score).

ST   Berlin, Staatsbibliothek zu Berlin, Mus. ms. Bach Stimmen (parts).

TWV   [Telemann-Werke-Verzeichnis.] Martin Ruhnke, ed. *Georg Philipp Telemann: Thematisch-Systematisches Verzeichnis seiner Werke: Instrumentalwerke.* 3 vols. Kassel: Bärenreiter, 1984–.

Bach the Cobbler

The Origins of J. S. Bach's
E-Major Concerto (BWV 1053)

Gregory Butler

In an earlier study on Bach's reception of the mature concertos of Tomaso Albinoni,[1] I established that the ritornello as well as certain compositional procedures in the third movement of J. S. Bach's Concerto for Cembalo Concertato and Strings in E Major (BWV 1053) were modeled on the third movement of Albinoni's Concerto for Two Oboes, op. 9 no. 4 (1722), music that Bach is unlikely to have encountered before he moved to Leipzig in May 1723. My findings appeared to confirm the position of scholars espousing the theory that a rather substantial portion of Bach's concerted chamber music had its origins during the Leipzig years,[2] particularly after 1729, when he took over the direction of the Collegium Musicum. Some scholars advocating pre-Leipzig origins for this music have glossed over my findings.[3] Partly because of the demonstrably late date of composition of the *Urform* of this movement during the period 1722–26, but also as a result of my analytical studies, I began to question the assumption that all three movements originated concurrently as the three movements of an earlier chamber concerto for solo melody instrument. In the following study, I will call on source studies as well as analytical evidence to shed light on the origins of the movements of this concerto.

Single movements or, in some cases, pairs of movements from the seven concertos and torso of an eighth preserved in the autograph score, P 234, exist in earlier ver-

1. See Gregory Butler, "J. S. Bach's Reception of Tomaso Albinoni's Mature Concertos," in *Bach Studies* 2, ed. Daniel R. Melamed (Cambridge, Mass.: Cambridge University Press, 1995), 20–46.

2. For example, see Christoph Wolff, "Bach's Leipzig Chamber Music," *Early Music* 13 (1985): 165–75, reprinted under the same title as Chapter 17 in Christoph Wolff, *Bach: Essays on His Life and Music* (Cambridge, Mass.: Harvard University Press, 1991), 223–38.

3. My essay is cited by Siegbert Rampe and Dominik Sackmann in the bibliography to their recent booklength study on Bach's concerted music, but nowhere are my findings addressed in their discussion either of the origins of BWV 1053 or of the chronology of BWV 1053/3, whose *Urform* they date to the same period as that of BWV 1053/1, namely, the early Köthen years. See BOM, 129–32, 217–28.

sions scored for obbligato organ as sinfonias, arias, or choruses in cantatas, primarily those from the third and fourth yearly cycles. BWV 1053 is a case in point; its three movements are also transmitted as cantata movements with organ obbligato—the first and second movements as the "Sinfonia" and aria "Stirb in mir, Welt" of the cantata *Gott soll allein mein Herze haben* (BWV 169), performed on the Eighteenth Sunday after Trinity in 1726 (October 20), and the third movement as the "Sinfonia" that opens the cantata *Ich geh und suche mit Verlangen* (BWV 49), performed two weeks later on the Twentieth Sunday after Trinity (November 3). BWV 169/1 is in D major and BWV 169/5 is in B minor, whereas BWV 49/1 is in E major, the same key as BWV 1053. In both sinfonias, woodwind instruments augment the ripieno strings—in BWV 169/1, two oboes d'amore and taille and in BWV 49/1, a single oboe d'amore.

Ulrich Siegele established that the cantata movements and the movements of the concerto, although they shared a common *Vorlage*, were independent of one another.[4] His argument that this common *Vorlage* was a three-movement concerto for solo melody instrument, widely accepted by Bach scholars, is perpetuated in the two most recent discussions of the source history of this work. Siegbert Rampe and Dominik Sackmann begin by stating categorically: "The *Vorlage* for the E-major harpsichord concerto is one of Bach's concertos which has disappeared,"[5] and in the recently published critical notes to the *Neue Bach-Ausgabe* edition of the concertos for solo cembalo, the editor, Werner Breig, concludes that "BWV 1053 on the one hand and the cantata movements BWV 169/1,5 and BWV 49/1 on the other, independently of one another, go back to a solo concerto for concertising melody instrument which has disappeared."[6]

Siegele's conclusion that this putative concerto was in the key of E♭ major[7] was based largely on such mechanical elements as range of the solo parts and failed to take into account important source evidence such as the transposition errors in the autograph scores of the two cantatas in question. This evidence is most unambiguous in the case of the aria "Stirb in mir, Welt," the version of the slow movement preserved in the autograph score of BWV 169, P 93. The organo obbligato part is notated in A minor, a tone lower than the other parts,[8] and all four corrections of transposition errors in

---

4. See KBT, 137.

5. "Die Vorlage des E-Dur-Cembalokonzerts ist eines von Bachs verschollenen Konzerten," BOM, 129.

6. ". . . BWV 1053 einerseits und die Kantatensätze BWV 169/1+5 und 49/1 andererseits unabhängig voneinander auf ein verschollenes Solokonzert mit konzertierendem Melodieinstrument zurückgehen." See Werner Breig, ed., NBA VII/4 (*Konzerte für Cembalo*), KB, 87.

7. See Siegele, KBT, 141–43.

8. In Bach's Leipzig sacred cantatas, the organ parts are notated a tone lower than the other parts to

the organo obbligato bass/continuo part[9] are of notes originally notated a step too high down by step.[10] In the same part, for the first note in m. 4, Bach initially entered an A♯. When he subsequently entered the correct pitch, G♯, he neglected to transpose the sharp sign down by step. Further, at the beginning of m. 16, where there is a change of system in the autograph score, Bach originally entered a key signature of two sharps on the staff for the organo obbligato bass/continuo part and subsequently crossed it out.[11] All indications are that at least the continuo part in the *Vorlage* from which this movement was transcribed was notated in B minor.

This conclusion is borne out by clear instances in both the continuo and cembalo concertato bass parts in BWV 1053/2, the version of this movement in C♯ preserved in P 234, of the correction of notes originally entered a step too low up by step.[12] This evidence is at its most graphic in the correction of the cembalo concertato bass part in the second half of m. 16. (See Examples 1a and 1b.) In the *ante correcturam* reading given in Example 1a, in the second half of m. 18 in the cembalo concertato bass part, Bach originally continued with the unvarying rhythmic pattern of eighth rest and two eighth notes established at the beginning of the movement, here clearly notated a step too low in B minor. He subsequently corrected his transposition error and in the process revised the passage, giving the *post correcturam* reading in Example 1b. This bears out the evidence presented with regard to the organo bass/continuo part in BWV 169/2, namely, that the common *Vorlage* from which Bach was transcribing both it and this version of the movement must have been pitched in B minor, and not C minor as Siegele argues.[13]

---

accommodate the Leipzig instruments, which, like most organs at the time, were tuned in *Chorton* and sounded a tone above the other instruments, tuned in *Cammerton*.

9. In the autograph scores of the three movements under consideration here, the bass part doubles as the continuo and the left hand of the obbligato organ parts.

10. Mm. 1,1–2; 4,1; 14,1; 22,2. A close examination of the third of these indicates clearly that the correction is not from a note originally notated a third too high, as suggested in the critical notes, but rather a second too high.

11. For documentation of these errors in transcription, see Matthias Wendt, ed., NBA I/24 (*Kantaten zum 18. und 19. Sonntag nach Trinitatis*), KB, 64–65.

12. M. 2,9 (violin 2); m. 4,4 (viola); m. 5,2 (continuo); m. 7,4 (violin 2); m. 10,1 (violin 1); m. 11,1 (violin 2); m. 16,5–8 (cembalo concertato bass); m. 24,4 (violin 2); m. 26,1 (cembalo concertato bass). The correction of a note originally entered a step too high down by step in m. 3,7 (violin 2) is not of a transposition error, but rather represents a revised reading, as both pitches are chord tones.

13. Rampe and Sackmann cite three corrections of transposition errors in BWV 1053/2 where the original pitch has been notated a step too low. See BOM, 131 and 465n22. They single out for special

Ante correcturam

19

Post correcturam

19

Ex. 1a, b. *Ante correcturam* and *post correcturam* readings at m. 183⁻4 in the Cembalo concertato bass part in the autograph score of BWV 1053/2, P 234.

The corrections of transposition errors or the lack of same in the ripieno parts and keyboard treble parts of BWV 169/5 and BWV 1053/2, although not quite so overwhelming, nevertheless point to a *Vorlage* in B minor. In the ripieno string parts in BWV 169/5 (notated in B minor), there is a single correction of a transposition error. This is of a note originally entered a step too high down by a tone,[14] whereas in the organo obbligato treble part, only one correction can be interpreted as a transposition error,[15] and it is of a note originally entered a step too high down by tone. In the ripieno string parts of BWV 1053/2, most of the corrections involve tinkering with voice leading, but the two corrections of transposition errors are of notes originally entered a step too low up by step.[16]

A correction in the autograph score of BWV 169/5 supports the general assumption that the original solo instrument in the common *Vorlage* from which this movement and BWV 1053/2 were transcribed was a melody instrument notated in the treble clef. Bach, in setting down the clefs at the beginning of the first system in the autograph

---

mention in the body of their text one of these, m. 13 (violin 1), which they refer to as "three connected notes" (drei zusammenhängende Töne). In fact, the three notes in question, the first, third, and fourth of four eighth notes in the measure, are not consecutive, and the corrections are from notes originally a fifth below, a fourth above, and a third below. See NBA VII/4, KB, 72. They are not corrections of transposition errors, but rather revisions of voice leading involving changes of chord tone. Further, one of the other corrections they cite, m. 6,1–3 (violin 2), is also not of a transposition error but involves a rhythmic revision. Nevertheless, their conclusion that the *Vorlage* from which Bach was transcribing BWV 1053/2 was pitched in B minor is valid (violin 2).

14. M. 32,1 (violin 2). There is thickening of noteheads at m. 24,3 (violin 2); m. 28,3 (violin 2); and m. 36,3 (violin 2) that cannot be interpreted as corrections of transposition errors.

15. M. 10,2.

16. M. 2,8 (violin 2); m. 3,7 (violin 2).

score, originally entered a treble clef at the beginning of the viola staff instead of the alto clef. This implies that in the source from which he was transcribing the top three clefs (in systems of five staves) were all treble clefs, the first for the solo instrument and the next two for the ripieno first and second violin parts. Thus the viola part occupied the fourth staff down in the *Vorlage* instead of the third, as it does in BWV 169/5.

Both the key of B minor and the range of two octaves from B to b' in the solo melody part of BWV 169/5 supports the oboe d'amore as the logical candidate for the solo melody part in the *Urform* of this movement. The range corresponds well with that of the oboe d'amore (A–b') but excludes both the oboe and transverse flute from consideration because the lowest note, B, exceeds the lowest playable note on either instrument. The restricted upper range, along with the fact that the *Urform* has been transposed up rather than down by a whole step in BWV 1053/2,[17] argues against the violin as a candidate for the solo melody instrument.[18]

If one had only the ripieno string parts in the autograph score of BWV 169/1 at one's disposal, one would be forced to conclude that Bach had transcribed the movement from a *Vorlage* in the key of D major, for these parts are clean in appearance—in fact, virtually free of corrections. But interestingly, when one examines the ripieno wind parts, one encounters a clear preponderance of corrections of transposition errors of notes originally notated a step too high down by step. In fact, these account for no fewer than sixteen[19] of the twenty-one corrections of transposition errors in the ripieno parts as a whole.

The unusual concentration of corrections of transposition errors in the ripieno wind parts can be explained by Bach's having transcribed the oboe 1, oboe 2, and taille parts as the top three staves of the autograph score of BWV 169/1 directly from the ripieno string parts in the *Vorlage* as the first stage in the process of adaptation. The errors in the ripieno wind parts made in the course of transcription were then corrected and the *post correcturam* readings were duplicated with minor adjustments in the three staves below as the violin 1, violin 2, and viola parts as a second, separate stage in the transcription process. Bach's adoption of this expedient for transcription

17. In every surviving *Urform* of a concerted work scored for solo violin(s), the arrangement for solo keyboard is pitched a whole tone lower.

18. However, one should not forget that in siciliano movements, scoring for solo violin amounts almost to a topos. For example, what is perhaps the most celebrated siciliano by Bach, the aria "Erbarme dich" from the *St. Matthew Passion*, scored for solo violin, alto, strings, and continuo, is in the key of B minor. As such, aside from the solo instrument, its scoring is virtually identical with that of BWV 169/5.

19. M. 13,1 (oboe 1); m. 19,2 (taille); m. 22,3 (taille); m. 23,3 (oboe 1); m. 30,7 (oboe 1 and violin 1); m. 50,4 (taille); m. 50,5 (taille); m. 52,2 (taille); m. 60,4 (taille); m. 75,2 (taille); m. 89,6 (oboe 2); m. 91,1 (taille); m. 104,7 (taille); m. 106,3 (oboe 2); m. 106,3 (taille); m. 106,5 (taille).

from the *Vorlage* would explain the relative paucity of such corrections in the ripieno string parts.

In a very few cases, Bach neglected to correct a transposition error in one of the ripieno wind parts and the transposition error was duly duplicated in the corresponding ripieno string part. For example, two notes originally entered a step too high in oboe 1 at mm. 30,7–31,1 went uncorrected during the first phase of the transcription process. Subsequently, when Bach came to enter the reading in violin 1 during the second phase, he entered the first note incorrectly but noticed the error immediately and corrected it before entering the correct reading for the second note. He must then have corrected the *ante correcturam* reading in oboe 1. From the foregoing, it is clear that the ripieno string parts in the *Vorlage* from which Bach was transcribing the ripieno wind parts in the autograph score of BWV 169/1 must have been pitched in E/E♭ major.[20]

The organo obbligato treble and organo obbligato bass/continuo parts of BWV 169/1 were entered into the autograph score after the ripieno wind and string parts as a unit. This is clear from Bach's having ruled the vast majority of the bar lines only through the upper six staves (those for the ripieno wind and string parts) and then continued them downward only later as he entered the organo obbligato treble and organo obbligato bass/continuo parts. In many cases, as, for example, in the bar lines at mm. 87–88 and 88–89, those for the lowest two staves bulge out noticeably to accommodate the thirty-second notes in these measures.

If in the *Vorlage* the solo melody and continuo parts were pitched in E/E♭ major, as my findings regarding the ripieno strings suggests, then the subsequent transposition of the movement into the key of D major in transcribing it as BWV 169/1 would in turn have necessitated the transposition of both the organo obbligato treble and bass/continuo parts down a major third into C major (D major Chorton). Consequently, one would expect to find in them corrections of transposition errors of notes originally notated a third too high down a third. In fact, there are two such corrections in the organo obbligato treble part.[21]

It is clear from the foregoing that in the common *Vorlage* from which Bach transcribed BWV 169/1, the ripieno instruments were originally pitched in E/E♭ major. Although there are three corrections of transposition errors in the ripieno string parts,

20. Matthias Wendt, although he acknowledges that in BWV 169/1 "corrections from the upper second are relatively frequent," concludes that "nonetheless, their number is not sufficient to substantiate the existence of a *Vorlage* in E major (or E♭ major)." (Korrekturen aus der Obersekunde relativ häufig sind, . . . ihre Anzahl reicht jedoch nicht aus, um auf eine Vorlage in E-Dur oder Es-Dur.) NBA I/24, KB, 76.

21. M. 43,1–2; m. 97,6–9.

all of notes originally entered a step too low up by step,[22] not a single correction can be interpreted as the result of a transposition error in either the cembalo concertato treble and bass or continuo parts in the version of the movement preserved in the autograph score of BWV 1053/1 in P 234. All indications are that the original solo melody instrument and basso continuo, like the ripieno strings, were originally notated at the same pitch, E/E♭ major. In the first of the two corrections of notes originally entered a third too high down by a third in the organo obbligato treble part in the autograph score of BWV 169/1, the F♯ beside the second of the two notes originally entered a third too high was an A♯, and in the second, the E♯ originally entered was subsequently corrected to C♯. The transposition downward, then, was by major third rather than minor third, so that the solo melody part in the *Vorlage* must have been notated in E major and not E♭ major.

As in the case of BWV 169/5, a correction of clef in the autograph score of BWV 169/1 offers indirect evidence that the *Urform* of BWV 169/1 was also scored for solo melody instrument, strings, and continuo. The bass clef mistakenly entered at the beginning of the system for the organo obbligato treble part at m. 103 suggests strongly that in the *Vorlage* from which Bach was transcribing this movement, the staff directly beneath the viola staff was allocated to the continuo part. This in turn suggests that the solo part in the *Urform* of this movement must have been for a melody instrument occupying the uppermost staff in systems of five staves.

The autograph score of the "Sinfonia" BWV 49/1 in the autograph score, P 111, presents a rather different picture. The correction of transposition errors in both the organo treble and organo bass/continuo parts in this source are unambiguous: eighteen of the twenty are of notes originally entered a step too high down by step.[23] The *Vorlage* from which this part was transcribed was clearly notated in E/E♭ major.

The decipherable corrections of transposition errors in the ripieno parts, virtually without exception, are of pitches originally entered a step too low up a tone.[24] Of particular interest here are the corrections of transposition errors in the oboe d'amore part. That Bach began the process of transcription by entering the top two staves comprising the oboe d'amore and violin 1 parts as a unit before entering the lower staves is clear from his discontinuous drawing of the bar lines in three stages (oboe d'amore

---

22. Violin 2, m. 32,5–6; violin 2, m. 46,1; violin 2, 55,4.

23. In the organo obbligato treble part, mm. 83,4; 87,6; 102,1; 116,1; 150,3; 190,3; 213,5; 231,1, and in the organo obbligato bass/continuo part, mm. 25,1; 41,1; 77,2–3; 90,1; 94,1; 96,1; 106,1; 160,1; 192,1; 232,1–3.

24. Oboe d'amore, m. 12,3; oboe d'amore, m. 49,1; violin 2, m. 107,2; oboe d'amore, m. 144,1; viola, m. 164,1; violin 1, m. 179,2; violin 2, m. 207,1; viola, m. 207,1; oboe d'amore, m. 226,1; viola, 238,1–4.

+ violin 1; violin 2 + viola; organo obbligato treble + organo obbligato bass/continuo). This is most notable when a bar line bulges out below the first two staves as at mm. 225–26, for example. All indications are that Bach followed the same process as he had in the case of BWV 169/1—that is, as the first stage of adaptation he transcribed the oboe d'amore part from the first violin part in the *Vorlage* and then duplicated it in the staff below as the violin 1 part in the transcribed version. This would explain why there are virtually no corrections of transposition errors in the violin 1 part, whereas there are several in the other two ripieno string parts.

Although the evidence of the correction of transposition errors in the ripieno parts might seem to point toward a *Vorlage* in D major, the number of corrections is relatively small when compared with that in the autograph score of BWV 169/1, and their interpretation as stemming from transposition errors in transcribing from a D-major *Vorlage* in every case is open to question, so that the situation here is far from unambiguous.

One possible interpretation of what seems to be conflicting evidence is that this movement was not transcribed from a single *Vorlage* but rather from two—one pitched in D major from which the ripieno parts were entered[25] and another in E/E♭ major from which the organo obbligato treble and bass/continuo parts were carried over. If the organo obbligato bass/continuo part in BWV 49/1 represents the continuo part of the *Vorlage*, then the only good explanation for its not having been transcribed from a D-major *Vorlage* along with the ripieno strings is that a keyboard part notated in *Cammerton* as a unit was transcribed from the E/E♭-major *Vorlage*. Although such a conclusion would seem to be counterintuitive, flying in the face of everything we know about Bach's transcription practices, the hypothesis, presented by Christoph Wolff elsewhere in this volume, of a Dresden performance of this movement for solo organ at *Cammerton* pitch would lend support to this scenario.

As for BWV 1053/3, both the cembalo concertato and the continuo parts in P 234 are virtually free of transposition errors, and only two corrections in the ripieno string parts may in any way be interpreted as corrections of transposition errors.[26] This movement gives every indication of having been transcribed from the same *Vorlage* in the key of E/E♭ major as the organo obbligato treble and organo obbligato bass/continuo parts in BWV 49/1.

The viola part (B 8) for this movement in the set of parts ST 55 is in D major, and

25. See Ulrich Bartels, ed., NBA I/25 (*Kantaten zum 20. und 21. Sonntag nach Trinitatis*), KB, 100.

26. The first, m. 49,1 (viola), is a pronounced enlargement of the notehead and thus could be interpreted as either the correction of a note originally entered a step too high or a step too low, or simply as a "thickened" (*verdickt*) notehead. The second, m. 163,2 (violin 2), the correction of a note originally entered a step too high, makes no sense in any context.

Ulrich Bartels has suggested that it was taken over from a *Vorlage* in that key.[27] That is, the scribe must have been copying from a preexistent D-major *Vorlage* rather than from the recently completed score of BWV 49/1 in E major.[28] Although this explanation would seem to clinch the argument for a D-major *Vorlage* from which the ripieno parts for this movement were transcribed, the situation is not quite so simple.

The scribe of this part, Johann Heinrich Bach, began by entering a bass clef with a key signature of one sharp before replacing it with the correct alto clef, partially overlying the original bass clef, with C♯ on the third line and time signature. All of the remaining staves have alto clef and a key signature of two sharps. The first two notes in m. 1 have been transposed—not corrected—up by a tone, the only time a reading correctly notated in D major has been transposed into the "wrong" key of E major. From this point on, there are six instances of notes or other accidentals originally entered either a third or a second too low[29] and seven of notes or accidentals originally entered a step too high.[30] However, it must be stated that two particularly prominent corrections in m. 199 and m. 233 would suggest that the scribe was copying from a *Vorlage* in E/E♭ major.

A single reading in m. 71 that diverges from that in the autograph score of both BWV 49/1 and BWV 1053/3.[31] However, the fact that at three points[32] mm. 26, 71–72, and 185, this part presents readings that correspond with *post correcturam* readings in P 111 and further, that a number of corrections of notes originally entered a step too high come between the end of one system and the beginning of the next in the autograph score, would seem to establish that B 8 was copied from the autograph score and not from a D-major *Vorlage*.[33]

To establish E♭ rather than E as the key of the *Urform* of either of the outer movements, evidence would have to be found in the autograph scores of transposition up by half step of notes originally entered a half step too low in the later versions in E major (BWV 1053/1,3, BWV 49/1) or transposition down by half step of notes originally

27. See NBA I/25, KB, 100.

28. It is unlikely that B 8 stems from an earlier set of parts, because the paper is consistent with that found in ST 55 as a whole.

29. Mm. 4,2; 28,5; 36,1; 66,1; 71,1; 163,2.

30. Mm. 37,1; 37,2; 124,1; 133,1; 199,2–3; 230,1; 233,1–2.

31. The copyist originally entered a–g as the first two notes and subsequently corrected the first note up by a tone. At the same point in the autograph score of BWV 49/1, the reading is a–b (E major).

32. Mm. 26,3; 71,1–2; m. 185,2–5.

33. Discussions with Joshua Rifkin about B 8 proved most instructive in allowing me to reject this source as evidence of a D-major *Vorlage* for this movement.

entered a half step too high in the one later version in D major (BWV 169/1). Of the latter, there are none while of the former three such corrections have been put forward as evidence of errors made as a result of transcribing from a *Vorlage* originally notated in E♭.[34] As I have already pointed to two prominent corrections of notes originally entered a major third too high down by major third in the organo obbligato treble part notated in C in the autograph score of BWV 169/1, a source in which there is absolutely no evidence suggesting that the *Vorlage* from which Bach was transcribing was in E♭, I would like to examine first a correction in the later version of the same movement in the autograph score of BWV 1053/1, that at m. 74,1. Here the natural sign has been superimposed on a symbol entered previously, but given the illegibility of the correction, whether that original symbol was a flat sign is not clear. so no conclusions one way or the other may be drawn from it.[35]

The pertinent correction in BWV 1053/3 occurs in the cembalo concertato treble part at m. 169,1 where a sharp sign corrects the natural sign entered originally. Because this correction occurs toward the end of a passage having B minor as its local tonic (mm. 164,3–168,3) replete with a D♮s and falls on the downbeat resolution of the seventh scale degree in a dominant seventh harmony, e♮, at the end of the preceding measure (m. 169,6), it is not at all certain whether it indeed represents an error of transcription. It is possible that the *Vorlage*, although notated in E major, may also have had a D♮ at this point as an alternate reading, with the D♯ arriving only subsequently with the last note of the same measure, or it may in fact have been originally entered as a D♯ that Bach, wavering on the tonal context initially entered as D♮. The same can be said of a correction in BWV 49/1 in P 111, that in the continuo part at m. 236,5, where again a sharp sign corrects a natural sign entered previously. Here the evidence speaks in favor of a transposition error of a note originally entered a half step lower, because the natural reading makes no sense whatever in the harmonic context of the passage in question. Although incontrovertible proof of an E♭ *Vorlage* for BWV 49,1 is open to question, the transposition errors discussed here lean in that direction.

As for the outer movements, there has been much debate as to the identity of the solo melody instrument, and the situation is far from clear. Many hold the original concertizing instrument to be the oboe, a position greatly promoted by recordings of the supposed *Urfassung* of BWV 1053 with oboe solo. With Stephen Hammer as soloist, Joshua Rifkin has recorded a reconstruction in E♭,[36] a key deemed by Bruce

34. I would like to thank Joshua Rifkin for bringing these to my attention in a communication of May 6, 2005.

35. Unfortunately, this is not clarified in NBA VII/4, KB, where the correction is not noted in the list of corrections for BWV 1053/1.

36. See *J. S. Bach, Oboe Concertos*, Pro Arte Digital PAD 153, Minneapolis, Minn., 1983. For a text of

Haynes to be "nicht instrumentengerecht" for the outer movements.[37] Haynes also concludes that performance of the solo part in F major on oboe is "keineswegs ideal," noting its shrill effect at the higher pitch. However, he goes on to note that for ease of execution, performance of the work in D major with oboe d'amore as the solo melody instrument is ideal.

Given the evidence pointing to *Vorlagen* for the outer movements in E/E♭ major and for the middle movement in B minor, only the outer movements can ever have originated in an earlier concerto. In the following analysis, I will demonstrate that the likelihood of both these movements having originated during Bach's first years in Leipzig is remote indeed.

To begin with, in BWV 1053/1 which is in da capo aria form, the A section (mm. 1–62) itself constitutes a fully formed, if diminutive, modified da capo aria form in which the B section (mm. 37–47) is not framed by identical statements of the A section but rather is inserted between the opening segment of the A section Aa up to the statement of the ritornello in the dominant (Aa) and the closing segment (Ab). (See Figure 1.)

This case, in which a self-sufficient modified da capo aria structure in turn forms the A section of the larger ABA da capo aria structure of the movement as a whole, is to be encountered nowhere else in Bach's ritornello form concerto movements. It is possible that Bach added the B section of the larger structure (mm. 63–113) when preparing BWV 169/1, perhaps to expand the earlier version of the movement and thus bring it into line with other concerted movements in da capo form he was composing at the time. If he did so, then the early version of the movement would ostensibly go back to the period during which Bach was experimenting with the adaptation of various aria structures to concerted movements, which seems to have culminated with such fully formed modified da capo aria forms as that represented by the third

---

this reconstruction, see Arnold Mehl, ed. (Edition Kunzelmann: Lottstetten/Waldshut and Adliswil/Zurich, 1983).

37. See Bruce Haynes, "Johann Sebastian Bachs Oboenkonzerte," BJ 78 (1992): 32. Beyond the generally unidiomatic nature of the part, Haynes points specifically to the "fast chromatic passages in mm. 161–75 and 243–58," which "specially in this tonality causes them to be performed badly on a woodwind instrument" (die schnellen chromatischen Gänge in T. 161–175 und 243–258 lassen sich gerade in dieser Tonart auf einem Blasinstrument schlecht ausführen). He goes on to point out that the key of E♭ major was by no means a common tonality for oboe concertos in the eighteenth century (thirty-four works in all) and that Bach himself uses this key in fewer than 5 percent of his oboe parts. He concludes by stating that "The historical grounds for the use of the tonality E♭ major are altogether unconvincing and the technical demands are, for me as player, suspect" (Die historischen Gründe für eine verwendung der Tonart Es-Dur sind insgesamt nicht überzeugend, und die technischen Anforderungen sind für mich suspekt).

Figure 1. Formal structures of the A sections of BWV 1053/1 and BWV 1053/3

BWV 1053/1 (C)

			A		B	Ab
			Aa			
measure	1–8	9–17	18–29	29–36	37–47	48–62
Solo–Tutti	T	S; S	T; S	T	S, T, S; S, T, S	T, S; T
tonality	I	I, V V	I V	V	vi iii	I, IV→I I

BWV 1053/3 (3/4)

			A		
measure	1–19	19–43	43–61	61–107	107–37
Solo–Tutti	T	S, T; S, S	T	S; T, S	T
tonality	I	I I,→V	V	V→I I	I

movement of the First Brandenburg Concerto (BWV 1046/3), a movement inserted into the early version of this concerto, BWV 1046a, ostensibly for a reperformance of the work in Köthen sometime before the compilation of the collection in the spring of 1721.[38] The diminutive proportions of the A section of BWV 169/1 suggest that it may have been composed considerably earlier, perhaps during the period 1713–17, when structures of similar proportions appear in arias from Bach's Weimar cantatas.

Given that the scenario described here is nothing more than a working hypothesis, are there other aspects of the gross formal structure of BWV 1053/1 that set it apart from Bach's later approach to ritornello concerto form in movements composed during the early Leipzig years, such as BWV 1053/3? The comparison of the gross formal structures of the A sections of these two movements indicates that besides the obvious presence of the inserted B subsection in BWV 1053/1, this movement contains a further additional period. The opening solo period (mm. 9–17), instead of modulating to the dominant and remaining there in preparation for the second statement of the ritornello in the same key, the procedure commonly followed by Bach in his da capo arias, after a single measure in the tonic moves quickly to the dominant (mm. 10–11), back to the tonic (mm. 12–13), and finally settles in the dominant (mm. 14–17). The period that follows consists not of a statement of the ritornello in the dominant as in BWV 1053/3, but opens with a statement of the initial segment of the ritornello in the tonic (mm. 18–23) before the second solo modulates to and cadences in the dominant

38. The third movement of the A-Major Concerto (BWV 1055), also in modified da capo aria form, is thought to have been composed circa 1720. For the dating of this work, see Hans-Joachim Schulze, "Johann Sebastian Bachs Konzerte—Fragen der Überlieferung und Chronologie," in *Bach Studien 6, Beiträge zum Konzertschaffen Johann Sebastian Bachs*, ed. Peter Ahnsehl, Karl Heller, Hans-Joachim Schulze (Leipzig, 1981), 13–15.

(mm. 24–29). It is only at this point with the fourth period that the full statement of the opening ritornello in the dominant occurs (mm. 29–37). This return to the tonic after the opening solo is a structural feature of at least one concerted movement composed in the late Weimar or Köthen period, the first movement of the Sixth Brandenburg Concerto (BWV 1051/1), in which the third period (mm. 25–28) begins on the dominant but, interpreted as a dominant seventh, then cadences strongly in the tonic. This has the result of attenuating the tonic harmony at the beginning of the structure and delaying the arrival in the dominant until the midpoint of the structure, at the same time limiting the concluding material in the tonic to less than a quarter of the total length of the structure. In BWV 1053/3, by contrast, the dominant is reached less than a third of the way through the structure and the concluding tonic segment, Ab, accounts for more than half of the section as a whole. The formal architecture and its effect in both cases is radically different.

An examination of the opening ritornellos of the two movements presents a similar disparity in approach. The ritornello that opens BWV 1053/1 does not begin immediately with the expected *Vordersatz* but with what in BWV 169/1 was originally a preparatory riff for violin 1 alone (mm. 1–2), here in the later version with accompaniment added. This introductory solo segment consists of an arpeggiated figure with its varied repetition. Such opening solo intonational introductions for violin 1 occur in at least two other concerto movements by Bach, the third movements of the D-Minor Concerto (BWV 1052/3) (m. 1) and the C-Minor Concerto (BWV 1060/3) (mm. 1–2). The former movement and the opening movement of the Fifth Brandenburg Concerto (BWV 1050a/1) are closely related through their solo cadenzas, which bear a striking structural resemblance to each other.

A direct, rather than indirect, link between BWV 1053/1 and BWV 1050/1 has to do with the second segments of their opening ritornellos (mm. 3–4). (See Example 2.)

Using BWV 169/1, which is in the same key as BWV 1050a/1, for purposes of demonstration, a comparison of the outer voices in these parallel passages indicates that both are built on the same bass progression—a scale in eighth notes descending from the tonic in the first measure that is repeated a third lower in the second measure. In the case of BWV 169/1, this descending scale is broken at the lower sixth by the eighth rest and repeated note, and in BWV 1050/1 it descends unbroken through the octave. In the second measure, instead of leaping up to the sixth scale degree as in BWV 169/1, the scalar descent in BWV 1050/1 continues to the leading tone, which then resolves to the tonic before leaping up a fourth to take up the repeated statement on the third note of the scale. As for the upper part, the first four eighths (broken into repeated sixteenth notes in BWV 1050a/1) in both cases are identical, whereas in the rest of the phrase the melody proceeds differently until the very end, where both have in common the rising seventh on the last two eighths of the second measure. The structural

Ex. 2. Outer Parts of BWV 169/1, mm. 3–4.

framework employed at analogous formal points in these two ritornellos, and found in no other concerto ritornello of Bach's, links these two movements closely.

A comparison of the compositional approach to the opening solo periods of the outer movements of BWV 1053 offers a striking contrast. (See Figure 2.) The opening solo period of BWV 1053/3 is a double *Devise* of the kind I have already identified elsewhere.[39] In the first of its two clauses, in the tonic throughout, it presents a strongly profiled solo segment or instrumental motto, *x* (mm. 19–22), followed by a tutti statement of the head motive segment, *y* (mm. 23–26), from the opening ritornello. The second clause begins with a restatement of the initial solo segment, *x* (mm. 27–30), harmonized differently, followed by an extended new solo segment, *z* (mm. 30–43), beginning with a sequential module modulating to the dominant and concluding with a module consolidating the new key and a cadential module. I have hypothesized that Bach began experimenting with the double *Devise* (a structure which he had already used in da capo arias) circa 1718 and that he then employed it more or less continuously in his solo concertos, with some modification, well into the Leipzig years.

The opening solo period of BWV 1053/1 also is made up of two clauses, but there the similarity with BWV 1053/3 ends. This is demonstrably not a double *Devise* structure, for it includes no statement of the incipit or the ritornello. The first clause is

39. See Gregory G. Butler, "The Question of Genre in J. S. Bach's Fourth Brandenburg Concerto," in *Bach Perspectives* 4, ed. David Schulenberg (Lincoln: University of Nebraska Press, 1999), 24–26. My diagram follows the format adopted in Table 5.

Figure 2. Formal structures of the opening solo periods of
BWV 1053/1 and BWV 1053/3

BWV 1053/1, mm. 9–17					
measure	| 9–13;	14–17	|		
Solo–Tutti	| S	S	|		
tonality	| I, V, I	V	|		
segment	| x	yz	|		

BWV 1053/3, mm. 19–43					
measure	| 19–22,	23–26;	27–30,	30–43	|
Solo–Tutti	| S	T	S	S	|
tonality	| I	I	I	→V,V	|
segment	| x	y	x	z	|

made up of a single solo segment, x (mm. 9–13), which shifts immediately into the dominant after only a single introductory measure in the tonic before moving back to the tonic at its close. The second clause begins abruptly in the dominant with a cursory solo segment, y (mm. 13–14), followed by an accompanied solo segment, z (mm. 14–17), consisting of a variation on the second segment of the opening ritornello (mm. 15–16) and a new cadential segment (m. 17). The shift at the outset to the dominant, and the somewhat aimless oscillation back and forth between tonic and dominant with extended middle-voice dominant pedal, that characterizes this structure is at odds with the approach in the double *Devise* of BWV 1053/3, where there is a prolongation of the tonic through the first half of the period, followed by a measured modulation to the dominant and consolidation of that key only in the closing measures of the period.

Furthermore, although there is a repetition of the opening solo segment and the opening ritornello segment is stated literally in BWV 1053/3, there is no exact restatement of any solo or tutti material in BWV 1053/1. All this imparts to the latter a rather free, almost improvisatory character. One should note in closing the clear articulation of the first three segments of the opening solo period in BWV 1053/3 into four-measure periods. There is no such periodic articulation in that of BWV 1053/1, which consists in two continuous clauses of five and three and a half measures' duration, respectively.

The concluding solo and tutti periods of these two A sections are also handled rather differently. (See Figure 1.) In BWV 1053/1, the two are fused into a single three-clause period consisting of a statement of the first three measures of the ritornello (mm. 48–50) broken off by the entry of the third solo (mm. 51–54), which opens in the subdominant and moves back to the tonic before concluding with a half close followed by the closing statement of the ritornello (mm. 56–62). The final full statement of the ritornello then acts as the logical completion of the truncated statement that opens the period. In BWV 1053/3 these two segments are articulated into two clear periods. The first, the second solo period (mm. 61–79), is in the tonic throughout and concludes with a full close. The concluding statement of the ritornello (mm. 107–25) is extended by a perorational clause (mm. 125–37) to form an epilogue unique in Bach's ritornello form concerto movements.

Even the brief and somewhat selective analysis given here should suffice to point to heterogeneous origins for the outer movements of BWV 1053. Just because these two movements appear as the sinfonias of two cantatas, BWV 169/1 and BWV 49/1, performed by Bach only two weeks apart is surely not to say that they must have been composed at the same time as Wolff argues.[40] On the contrary, the opening movement appears to have been written in the orbit of the early version of the Fifth Brandenburg Concerto (BWV 1050a),[41] at a time when Bach was perhaps at the beginning of an extended period of experimentation in applying various aria structures to ritornello concerto movements, the result of his intensive engagement with the aria in his Weimar cantatas. One might, on this basis, hazard a dating of this movement to the period 1714–17, a decade or so before the composition of BWV 1053/3.

Whatever else the evidence presented in the foregoing study indicates, it is clear that the common *Urform* of BWV 169/5 and BWV 1053/2 was in the key of B minor, and that of BWV 169/1 and BWV 1053/1 was in the key of E major. These two movements can thus never originally have constituted the first and second movements of an integral three-movement cycle. Rather, like the *Urform* of BWV 1056/1 (ostensibly a concerted movement for solo violin in G minor) and that of BWV 1056/2 (a concerted movement for solo oboe in F major), their origins must be considered to be entirely distinct from each other.

The common *Urform* of BWV 49/1 and BWV 1053/3 may not have originated as the closing movement of a concerto but rather as a sinfonia for solo melody instrument and strings opening a chamber cantata composed sometime during the two and a half years after Bach's arrival in Leipzig. Given the text of BWV 49, with its richly dense wedding allusions and its use of "Hautbois d'amour," the hypothesis that this movement represents an instrumental parody of the sinfonia to a wedding cantata is an attractive one.

Another plausible source, one that is highly intriguing in light of Bach's concertizing activities in the mid-1720s, is the "diversen Concerten" mentioned in the news-

---

40. See page 114 in this volume.

41. Pieter Dirksen has argued persuasively that BWV 1050a was written for Bach's visit to the Dresden court in the fall of 1717, in connection with the celebrated keyboard duel with Louis Marchand that failed to materialize. See Dirksen, "The Background to Bach's Fifth Brandenburg Concerto," in *Proceedings of the International Harpsichord Symposium Utrecht 1990* (Utrecht, 1992), 157–85.

paper account of a concert given by Bach on the Silbermann organ of the Dresden Sophienkirche on September 21, 1725,[42] a date that accords well with the time frame established for the composition of this movement.[43] The fact that the Silbermann organ was pitched in *Cammerton*[44] rather than the more usual *Chorton* would explain why the solo organ part in my hypothetical E/E♭-major *Vorlage* was notated in the same key as the ripieno instruments and not a tone lower in *Chorton*. Bach would then have had to transpose this *Cammerton* organ part into *Chorton* for the performance in the two principal Leipzig churches.[45]

The evidence I have presented establishing as the *Urform* for BWV 169/5 and BWV 1053/2 a movement for solo melody instrument (oboe d'amore?), strings, and continuo in B minor contradicts the hypothesis presented elsewhere in this volume by Christoph Wolff, which posits an integral D-major concerto for solo organ composed in September 1725 for Bach's Dresden recital as *Urform*. However, his argument that the slow movement originated in Leipzig during the period 1724–25 is compelling. If his suggestion that Bach performed three-movement concertos at the Dresden performance and not isolated movements is correct, it raises the possibility that Bach, in preparing repertory for this performance, brought together (1) an earlier concerted movement for solo melody instrument originally in E major composed in the late Weimar years, BWV 1053/1a, which he expanded in order to make it compatible with the more extended da capo structures he was exploring in ritornello allegro movements of the early Leipzig years; (2) an up-to-date slow "Siciliano" concerted movement for melody instrument originally in B minor, BWV 1053/2a, written recently in the style of similar arias from the period 1724–25; and (3) an allegro concerted movement scored from the outset for solo organ and strings in E/E♭ major, BWV 1053/3a, composed expressly for the Dresden concert of September 1725. This possibility supposes a further layer in the source history of this movement, at least for the opening two movements.

I think we must entertain the possibility that BWV 1053 was assembled from at least

---

42. For the complete report, see BDOK II, 150. The organ, completed by Gottfried Silbermann in November 1720, was tuned in *Cammerton*, and so the solo organ part would have been notated at the same pitch as the ripieno strings.

43. Christoph Wolff has already put forward the concerted movements that formed a part of the repertory for this and, no doubt, other similar concerts as an important source for the sinfonias for obbligato organ that open a number of the church cantatas composed between 1726 and 1728, citing BWV 1053 as "a prime candidate." See Christoph Wolff, *Johann Sebastian Bach: The Learned Musician* (New York: W. W. Norton, 2000), 318.

44. For the pitch of the Frauenkirche organ, see Ulrich Dähnert, *Historische orgeln in Sachsen* (Frankfurt-am-Main: Verlag das Musikinstrument, 1980), 86.

45. For an intriguing interpretation of this evidence bearing on the transposition of BWV 169/1 down a tone into D major, see p. 112 in this volume.

three heterogeneous sources, not linked to any putative earlier concerto *Urform*. In fact, my extended research on the origins of the concertos indicates that for Bach, such cobbling together of concertos from heterogeneous movements of different provenance was not exceptional.[46] My findings raise a number of issues around the question of the reconstruction of Bach's concerted movements as concertos for solo melody instrument. Given the heterogeneous origins of the movements of BWV 1053 and the difficulty of knowing for certain what solo melody instrument originally played the solo parts, are we then justified in arranging them as "original versions" at all? Or, true to the not improbable heterogeneous origins of the outer movements and Bach's later arrangements of them as sinfonias, should we not simply present them, even though out of context, as single movements, for example, to open concerts of chamber music?

For those who may feel justified in cobbling together their own concertos for melody instrument as Bach himself did for his later arrangements of disparate concerted movements as concertos for cembalo solo/concertato, strings, and continuo, choosing both key and instrument for a "BWV 1053a" is problematic, given that the *Vorlage* for the slow movement was in B minor, whereas those for the outer movements were in E and E/E♭ major, respectively. Scholarly reconstructions of hypothetical concertos when no *Urform* exists remain a highly risky venture at best, unethical at worst, and one must seriously question the advisability of the decision to sanction such reconstructions made by the editorial board of the *Neue Bach-Ausgabe*.[47]

The prevailing general view that those of the concertos for one, two, and three harpsichords, BWV 1052–64, for which the *Vorlagen* do not survive must represent arrangements of integral three-movement concerto cycles that have been lost is called into question at every turn by both external and internal source evidence suggesting that many of these concertos were cobbled together from single movements or pairs of movements. I believe strongly that one should exercise extreme caution in approaching virtually every concerto of Bach's. We should never assume that the *Urform* of the work in question is an integral three-movement cycle but should be aware that we may well be dealing with an assemblage, perhaps of three independent movements of stylistically, chronologically, and generically quite disparate origins.

Of the generically disparate origins of such isolated concerted movements, a lost

---

46. A chapter titled "Bach the Cobbler: The Origins of the Concertos," from my monograph on the origins and chronology of Bach's concerted chamber music now in preparation, deals at length with the disparate origins of the movements of the vast majority of those concertos for which the *Urform* has not survived.

47. I am referring here to the volume of concerto reconstructions, NBA VII/7 (*Verschollene Solokonzerte in Rekonstruktionen*), ed. Wilfried Fischer.

concerto is but one possibility and often the least likely. Among the most probable, I believe, are the sinfonias to both church and chamber cantatas. Bach seems to have recycled earlier cantata sinfonias to fill the same role later in Leipzig, particularly in the cantatas of the third and fourth yearly cycles, a practice akin to, and sometimes clearly a part of, the parody process. Just as vocal movements of chamber cantatas were normally lost to posterity once they had received a single performance, so the sinfonias to such works were subject to the same fate. It should come as no surprise, then, that the instrumental sinfonias, like the choruses and arias from occasional chamber cantatas, were parodied by Bach in his Leipzig church cantatas.

These isolated sinfonias could then do double duty, as a source of concerted movements for the chamber concertos Bach assembled beginning in the early Leipzig years. A prime example is his reuse of the sinfonia BWV 1046a/1 both as the basis for the first, second, and fourth movements of the First Brandenburg Concerto (BWV 1046) and then almost five years later for the "Sinfonia" that opens the cantata *Falsche Welt, dir trau' ich nicht* (BWV 52), performed on the Twenty-third Sunday after Trinity in 1726 (November 24). (In this case it is important that BWV 52/1 is clearly derived from the earlier of the two pre-Leipzig versions of this work, the first movement of the sinfonia BWV 1046a/1 without violino piccolo concertato, and not from the later Köthen version, the opening movement of the First Brandenburg Concerto.) It now seems clear that beginning around 1726, Bach went back to earlier Leipzig and pre-Leipzig sinfonias and arranged them for obbligato organ for reuse as cantata sinfonias and then later, having taken over as director of the Leipzig Collegium Musicum, assembled them, in some cases with newly composed concerted movements, into concertos for harpsichord(s) and strings.

Although he arranged Leipzig and pre-Leipzig sinfonias as the sinfonias for obbligato organ from the period 1726–28, there is not a single known case of Bach ever having recycled a movement of an earlier concerto (where that movement did not in turn have its origins in an earlier sinfonia) later as the sinfonia to a cantata. That is, the sinfonias from Bach's later Leipzig cantatas, although they may have been recycled subsequently as concerto movements, never themselves have their origins in concerto movements. This may well have to do with the particular function of the sinfonia as a preludial genre distinct from that of the concerto. Preludes for solo instrument could perfectly well be adapted to the role of cantata sinfonia because the two types were generically and functionally compatible. Following this line of reasoning, Bach would have thought of sinfonia and concerto as somewhat distinct generic entities, and he might have considered movements from concertos to be ill suited rhetorically to function as the *exordia* to cantatas.

The more one delves into the origins of these works, the more one has the feeling that the prehistories of virtually all of Bach's concertos, far from being straightforward, are fraught with complexity. Of course, the concertos are not unique in this respect. The evidence suggests that the origins of Bach's sonatas are no less complex and indeed, that in virtually every genre, he was constantly recycling movements and reassembling them depending on need and circumstance. Joshua Rifkin has stated the case against the existence of hypothetical concerto *Urformen* and in doing so supports the idea of Bach's cobbling together concertos from single movements:

> Scholars have generally read the fragmentary transmission of Bach's instrumental music as a sign that his production in this domain originally encompassed a far greater number of compositions than we can account for today. Surely, however, the very intensity with which Bach recycled his instrumental works tells us precisely the opposite—that he in fact wrote only a limited number of such pieces, which he then had constantly to adapt to ever new situations.[48]

Bach was not a Vivaldi who sat down and dashed off a concerto from scratch at a single sitting. The more we understand his creative process, his recourse to the process of *assemblage* by which he fashioned works by drawing together and recasting stylistically and chronologically heterogeneous movements, the more we realize that Bach, like his contemporaries, was highly practical and pragmatic. Not only was composition perhaps not as easy for him as we assume it was, but he was also constantly pressed for time. In retrospect, we view with some dismay early Bach scholars' shock on discovering that almost all the choruses and arias of the B-Minor Mass had been parodied from cantatas. It should come as no surprise to find that so many of Bach's concertos are similarly the fruits of this endlessly rich and imaginative parody process.

48. See Joshua Rifkin, "The 'B minor Flute Suite' Deconstructed: New Light on Bach's Ouverture BWV 1067," in *Bach Perspectives* 6 (Urbana: University of Illinois Press, 2005), 66–67.

J. S. Bach's Violin Concerto
in G Minor

Pieter Dirksen

Johann Sebastian Bach's concertos for solo cembalo (BWV 1052–59), preserved together in the autograph score P 234 (ca. 1738),[1] are, without exception, transcriptions of concertos for solo treble instruments. For seven of the concertos, the *Urform* has either been preserved—BWV 1054 (BWV 1042), BWV 1057 (BWV 1049), BWV 1058 (BWV 1041)—or the original solo instrument can be determined without difficulty—BWV 1052 (violin), BWV 1053 (oboe or oboe d'amore), BWV 1055 (oboe d'amore), BWV 1059 (oboe).[2] However, in the case of the F-Minor Concerto

The present text is a thorough revision and updating of a shorter German version of this essay, completed in 1993, which has circulated since that time in manuscript form among several Bach scholars. My theory concerning BWV Anh. I 2 has already been cited by Werner Breig ("Zur Werkgeschichte von Bachs Cembalokonzert BWV 1056," in BOW, 267 and in notes to the recording *Johann Sebastian Bach: Solo Concertos 1* [*Musica Alta Ripa*], MDG 309, 0681–2 [1996]). I wish to thank Werner Breig as well as Joshua Rifkin for their comments and, finally, David J. Smith (University of Aberdeen) for correcting my English.

1. Yoshitake Kobayashi, "Zur Chronologie der Spätwerke Johann Sebastian Bachs," BJ 74 (1988): 41.

2. See KBT, 130–31, 136–45; Wilfried Fischer, ed., NBA VII/7 (*Verschollene Solokonzerte in Rekonstruktionen*), KB, 36–40 (BWV 1052), 63–65 (BWV 1055), 132–37 (BWV 1053), and 138–40 (BWV 1059). Separately, concerning BWV 1053, see Joshua Rifkin, liner notes, Pro Arte PAD 153 (1983). The solo melody part of the original version of BWV 1055 has repeatedly been ascribed to the viola d'amore from Wilhelm Mohr, "Hat Bach ein Oboe-d'amore-Konzert geschrieben?" *Neue Zeitschrift für Musik* 133 (1972): 507–8 to BOM, 133–42. The discussion concerning BWV 1055 hinges on the question of whether the arpeggios in the cembalo part accompanying the ritornello of the first movement form an integral part of the piece. An examination of this elaboration in P 234 clearly indicates it to have been an afterthought crammed into the cembalo system after all of the other parts had been transcribed. Also inexplicable is the dichotomy between the three-octave range of the arpeggios (e–d''') and the two-octaves-plus-one-note compass (a–b'') observed everywhere else in the concerto's solo part. There would simply have been no reason for Bach to restrict himself to such a narrow compass in the solo part if the ostensible "viola d'amore compass" outlined by the arpeggios were available to him everywhere else. Beyond that, the arpeggios in question are, in fact, far more idiomatic on a keyboard than on a string instrument. I feel justified, therefore, in referring to BWV 1055[a] throughout this study as a work for oboe d'amore.

(BWV 1056), the identity of the original solo melody instrument is not so clear. The fact that its middle movement also appears in a much less ornamented form as the Sinfonia for solo oboe, strings, and continuo that opens the cantata *Ich steh mit einem Fuß im Grabe* (BWV 156) has generated a remarkably tenacious secondary tradition—that BWV 1056 represents a transcription of a lost oboe concerto.[3] However, Wilhelm Rust, in his edition of the work for the Bach Gesellschaft in 1867,[4] recognized the violinistic nature of much of the solo part of the concerto, and the matter was further clarified in studies by Ulrich Siegele and Wilhelm Fischer, who demonstrated that the origins of BWV 1056 lie not in a single concerto, but rather in two such works.[5] Following their argument, the outer movements have their origins in a violin concerto in G minor and the slow movement, in an oboe concerto for which the sinfonia BWV 156/1 represents a version much closer textually to the original than BWV 1056/2. Joshua Rifkin subsequently shed light on the source history of the slow movement,[6] demonstrating that neither BWV 1056/2 nor the cantata sinfonia represents the original version of this movement. He concluded that both versions go back to a lost version that formed the middle movement of an oboe concerto in D minor. According to Rifkin, the outer movements of this concerto have been preserved as the two sinfonias with obbligato organ that open the first and second parts of the cantata *Geist und Seele wird verwirret* (BWV 35). The fragment BWV 1059, based on the same lost model as BWV 35/1, suggests that Bach intended to arrange Rifkin's putative D-minor oboe concerto (BWV 1059[a]) for solo cembalo in its entirety.

More recently, however, the discussion about the genesis of these concertos and concerto movements has been revisited. Not only has doubt been cast on Rifkin's thesis of a lost D-minor oboe concerto, but further, the argument that the outer movements of BWV 1056 were originally connected has been refuted.[7] The present study will attempt to carry forward the discussion of BWV 1056, beginning with an investigation of the nature of the connection between its outer movements both from the perspec-

---

3. More recent examples can be found in Malcolm Boyd, *Bach* (London: Dent and Sons, 1983), 176. Boyd states that "the outer movements of the well known f-minor concerto (BWV 1056) are thought to have originated in a lost oboe concerto" and thus turns the facts upside-down. The work list in both editions of the entry "J. S. Bach" (Christoph Wolff et alia), in *New Grove* (1980, 2001), goes even one stage further by stating "outer mov[emen]ts from lost ob[oe] conc[erto], reconstructed in NBA VII/vii [*sic*]." See also *J. S. Bach: Konzert G-moll für Oboe und Orchester*, ed. Winfried Radeke (Wiesbaden: Breitkopf & Härtel, 1970).

4. See Wilhelm Rust, ed., BDOK XVII, *Vorwort*, xiv.

5. KBT, 128–30; NBA VII/7, KB, 81–86.

6. Joshua Rifkin, "Ein langsamer Konzertsatz Johann Sebastian Bachs," BJ 64 (1978): 140–47.

7. Bruce Haynes, "Johann Sebastian Bachs Oboenkonzerte," BJ 78 (1992): 37–38; BOM, 121–26 (BWV 1059[a]) and 142–45 (BWV 1056[a]).

tive of their instrumentation and of their formal structures. The restored outline of a G-minor violin concerto that emerges will then be linked to a surviving fragment of a slow concerted movement, and finally, the question of the work's chronology will be taken up.

The Solo Part in BWV 1056/3

The extensive correction of transposition errors by Bach demonstrates clearly that, like the other violin concertos arranged for cembalo concertato/solo in P 234 (BWV 1054, 1057, 1058), the outer movements of BWV 1056 were transcribed from an *Urform* pitched a tone higher in G minor.[8] In the case of the first movement, the range of the solo part in G minor, g–e''', the bariolage passage involving the open G-string (mm. 47–54), and the melody of the cadential extension at the close of the ritornello, clearly designed to end in the violins on their lowest playable note, g, leaves no doubt that the solo melody instrument in the *Urform* is the violin.[9] On the other hand, opinion is divided with regard to the third movement. Whereas Fischer and Breig accept the violin as the solo instrument in the original version of this movement, as well,[10] Bruce Haynes has claimed this movement for the oboe.[11] It is true that the treble line of the harpsichord when transposed to G minor never goes below c', the lowest note playable on the oboe, and that figuration idiomatic to the violin, such as the bariolage found in the first movement, is absent here. However, the G-minor version of the solo part reaches e♭''' in mm. 173–78, a note that is unplayable on the oboe but that in the solo parts of Bach's violin concertos is common in third position (e.g., BWV 1041–43, 1049). Haynes argues that the entire passage leading to these high notes (mm. 165–83) originally stood an octave lower, citing as proof the *ante correcturam* reading at the beginning of this passage in the autograph score (mm. 165–67), which indeed stands an octave lower.[12] (See Example 1.)

However, from a compositional perspective, it is unlikely that this really reflects the original reading, as both Siegele and Haynes have assumed. As Wilfried Fischer has observed, "Bach probably wanted to place these measures in a more favorable range for the cembalo but because of the ripieno parts, decided to return to the original pitch of the model."[13] A comparison with the parallel passage (mm. 73–90) suggests that Fischer's view is correct. The solo part at mm. 165–83 must sound above the ripieno

8. Werner Breig, ed., NBA VII/4 (*Konzerte für Cembalo*), KB, 146–47, 159.

9. See note 2 and BOM, 142.

10. NBA VII/7, KB, 81–82; Werner Breig, "Zur Werkgeschichte," 267.

11. Haynes, "Bachs Oboenkonzerte," 37.

12. KBT, 130; NBA VII/4, KB, 153.

13. NBA VII/7, KB, 95.

Ex. 1. BWV 1056[a]/3, mm. 178–84, comparison of "violin" and "oboe" versions

voices to differentiate itself from them, but in the "oboe" version, the solo part appears below both of the ripieno violins. It should also be noted that the first appearance of this material at mm. 73–90 lies comfortably high in the solo instrument, and thus the effect of repeating the entire passage in a lower register instead of a higher one would have been ineffective structurally. In addition, the hypothetical oboe version results in a musically implausible reading at m. 183 in the solo part.[14] As will be demonstrated later in this chapter, the climactic effect of the high e♭''' as the structural high point of this movement is destroyed if the passage in which it appears is pitched an octave lower. Moreover, it should be emphasized both that this is the same as the highest

14. In my opinion, Haynes's view that the transposition "does not affect what is musically meant" ("Bachs Oboenkonzerte," 37) is debatable.

pitch reached in the first movement and that it occurs at the same point structurally in both movements, namely in the last solo section at a penultimate climactic juncture.

There is another compositional argument to be advanced in favor of the violin as solo melody instrument in this movement. In the two corresponding antiphonal passages between solo instrument and ripieno (mm. 99ff, 203ff), the contrast between the monophonic solo statement as played by oboe and the full chords in the ripieno parts seems excessive. The cembalo version here has full four-part harmonies, and these should be seen as an accurate reflection of the original solo part rather than an adaptation as part of the transcription process. This view is borne out by a consideration of the compositional context, as well as by analogy with two similar passages in Bach's concerto oeuvre. (See Examples 2a, 2b, and 2c.)

The antiphonal passage develops a simple echo idea found in the initial ritornello

Ex. 2a. BWV 1056[a]/3, mm. 7–8

Ex. 2b. BWV 1056[a]/1, mm. 3–4

Ex. 2c. BWV 1060a/1, m. 2

segment *a'* (Example 2a). Here the echo appears in the ripieno strings as a simple repetition, without continuo accompaniment of the preceding measure with the top part transposed to the lower octave. There is increasing tension with both recurrences of *a'*. Here the repetition is not at the lower octave, and the two-measure segment cited in Example 2a expands to become a six-measure period in which the harmonic and melodic tension increase every two measures (see Example 3).

A comparison with the echo writing found in the opening ritornellos of the first movements of BWV 1056 (Example 2b) and the Concerto for Two Cembali, Strings, and Continuo in C Minor (BWV 1060) (Example 2c) is also revealing. In these works, the echoes involve only the last two eighth notes of a preceding ripieno phrase, a minimal portion of the measure, and Bach accordingly states them without harmonic support in the solo cembalo versions. In BWV 1056/3, on the other hand, the echo effects take up a whole measure and the "question" and "answer" segments of what amounts to a dialogue are demarcated by rests and fully harmonized. The chords of the harpsichord version must therefore be considered an integral part of the extended "dynamic" version of this passage. Consequently, the violin, capable of producing a polyphonic texture, is the only viable candidate as the solo melody instrument in the original version of the movement.[15] This conclusion is buttressed by the fact that during the tutti chords in the ripieno strings, the cembalo part is limited to two-part texture, whereas in the unaccompanied measures, the texture is expanded to include

15. NBA VII/7, KB, 94.

four parts.[16] This textual regulation of dynamics clearly demonstrates that Bach wanted to avoid a simple echo effect in favor of an antiphonal effect.

Fischer's reconstruction of the two passages employing multiple stops in the solo part may be improved on in one important respect, an improvement that confirms the compositional necessity for multiple stops. He overlooks the fact that the harmonic progression is built on a bass pedal point (reflected in the cembalo bass part) that should be retained in any reconstruction of the solo violin part. What is more, idiomatic violin writing not only allows for the harmonization of the repetition of the phrase for violin 1, but also for the incorporation an octave higher of the characteristic pedal-point octaves in the continuo part.

Fischer's view that the solo violin does not participate in the tutti chords of mm. 101, 103, 205, and 207 is also questionable. These chords are an extension of the preceding ritornello, and it would be acoustically unsatisfactory, especially in view of the minimal ripieno complement implied in the fast movements, if the solo violin were to drop out here. Again, any reconstruction for solo violin should follow more closely the cembalo treble part, which continues to double violin 1 at this point. Examples 3a and 3b present a hypothetical reconstruction of the two passages discussed here.

Further, it is likely that the fermata in the solo part at m. 196 originally had the double stop d'–c"–a", an obvious reading in this context and one that is eminently playable for the violin. Musically, such a reading would be imperative after the dynamic rise in tension during the preceding pedal-point figuration (mm. 183–96). A similar passage in the third movement of the A-Minor Violin Concerto (BWV 1041) has just such a double stop (e'–d"–b") at m. 90.[17]

The passage in the continuo part at mm. 136–46 in the last movement is also problematic in Fischer's reconstruction. He assumes that the cembalo bass part represents the original continuo part.[18] But as it appears in P 234, it clearly represents a revised reading dependent on the support of the continuo part (note the numerous implausible second-inversion harmonies that appear in mm. 138 and 144 of Fischer's reconstruction). The imitation between the cembalo bass and continuo parts in mm. 141–42 and 147–48 does not present a real problem, as the sixteenth notes in mm.

---

16. The score copied by Johann Nikolaus Forkel (P 239) in all probability reflects yet a further stage in Bach's revision process as carried out in the lost original set of parts (on this, see NBA VII/4, KB, 156–57 and 160). In P 234, on the other hand, the chords in some of the ripieno measures in this passage appear in the cembalo treble part, as well.

17. It should be noted, however, that in contrast to the corresponding point in BWV 1058/3, this chord is not present in the version for solo cembalo.

18. NBA VII/7, KB, 95.

Ex. 3a. BWV 1056[a]/3, violino concertato, mm. 98–104

Ex. 3b. BWV 1056[a]/3, violino concertato, mm. 202–8

142 and 148 of the continuo part clearly form an elaboration of the transcription in the cembalo bass part. This is also obvious from the diastematic alteration of the last sixteenth note of this revised reading, which differs from the original version at mm. 136, 141, 147 (cembalo bass), mm. 137, 143 (violin 1), mm. 138, 144 (violin 2), and 140, 146 (cembalo treble). Consequently, the passage in the continuo part in question might be reconstructed as shown[19] in Example 4.

All in all, it is evident that the two double-stopped pedal-point passages formed an integral part of the solo part in the *Urform* and that originally it had the typical ambitus of the violin, a–e♭''', which corresponds rather closely with that of the solo part in the first movement.

Finally, there are two more general but no less important arguments to be made against assigning the original solo part of this movement to the oboe. Only concerted movements originally scored for solo violin required downward transposition by a tone when subsequently arranged for keyboard. Had the solo part of this movement originally been scored for solo oboe, Bach would not have transposed it down a tone in arranging it for cembalo, because parts originally for solo woodwind instruments could be transcribed directly for the keyboard at pitch, as BWV 35 (BWV 1059), BWV 1055, and BWV 1060 demonstrate. Second, accepting disparate origins for the outer movements requires one to accept in turn that not only has the concluding movement of a violin concerto in G minor been lost, but also that no trace whatsoever exists of the first two movements of an oboe concerto in the same key. From the general perspective

19. In the first movement, there is another questionable passage in Fischer's otherwise admirable reconstruction. The half-measure rest between the unison conclusion of the ritornello and the solo entry in m. 21 is atypical of Bach, and the bridge consisting of triplet figuration in the cembalo part of BWV 1056 at this point must definitely reflect the original continuo part and should be restored in BWV 1056[a].

Ex. 4. BWV 1056[a]/3, continuo, mm. 136–46

of Bach's concerto oeuvre, with its closely knit network of arrangements and reuse of material, this must be considered as highly unlikely.[20] If one adds to this the fact that the outer movements of BWV 1056 are closely related in terms of dimension, form, and content and were clearly conceived as complementary, their having originated independently of one another can be safely ruled out.[21] Everything considered, then, one may assume that both outer movements were written originally for the violin and stem from the same lost concerto in G minor.

An Analysis of the Outer Movements

The outer movements of BWV 1056 are both cast in ritornello form. The concluding movement has a more traditional structure (see Example 5a) in which, in contrast to the opening movement, the ritornello material is played exclusively by the ripieno instruments. The ritornello of BWV 1056/3 can be viewed as a harmonized two-voiced framework with a clearly recognizable tripartite structure consisting of three segments, each comprising two four-measure phrases that might be termed antecedent (*aa'*, mm. 1–8), consequent (*ba''*, mm. 9–16), and epilogue (*b'c*, mm. 17–24).[22] (See Figure 1.)

But from the outset of the ensuing first solo episode, a less traditional aspect of

20. Haynes recognizes this problematic aspect of his theory, admitting: "Strangely, no complementary pieces are to be found for the third movement in order to arrive at a reconstruction of a complete [oboe] concerto" ("Bachs Oboenkonzerte," 38). See the similar argumentation regarding BWV 1059(a) in Rifkin, "Ein langsamer Konzertsatz Bachs," 146–47 and, on this aspect in general, in Joshua Rifkin, "Verlorene Quellen, verlorene Werke—Miszellen zu Bachs Instrumentalkomposition," in BOW, 67–79.

21. It is even more incredible to suggest that they originated as sinfonias to (Köthen?) cantatas (BOM, 144 and 435), which would surely represent a "stopgap" solution. There is no evidence whatsoever that Bach ever composed such typically concerto-like movements for solo melody instrument as introductions to his cantatas, and the contradictory examples ostensibly of Weimar origin cited by Rampe and Sackmann (BWV 31/1, 152/1, and 182/1) only tend to emphasize the strict differentiation observed by Bach.

22. I have adopted the terminology *antecedent* and *consequent*, with the addition of *epilogue*, as the English equivalents of the German terminology, *Vordersatz*, *Nachsatz*, and *Epilog*, usefully applied in

Figure 1. Formal analysis of BWV 1056/3

mm.	no.	ritornello	solo	tonal area*
1–24	24	*aa' ba" b' c*		**I** [→III→i]
25–48	24	[*a*]	*A*, with built-in ritornello fragment *a*	i→III
49–72	24	*aa'–ba"*	*a'* extended with built-in solo	**III**
73–92	20			iv→v
93–112	20	*aa'–b'c*	*a'* extended by organ point and solo interjections, *b"* with added solo line	**V/v**
113–36	24	[*a*]	*A*, with built-in ritornello fragment *a*	v→VII
137–48	12		*dialogue* between ripieno and solo based on *a*	VII→III–VI→ii/i
149–164	16	*aa'ba"*	solo line added to *a'b"*	**iv**
165–196	32		*B*, extended with pedal point figuration	VII→V/i→ →
197–224	28	*aa'–ba"b'c*	extended by organ point and solo interjections, *ba b* with added solo line	**i** [→III → i]

*main tonal areas in bold type

this concerto movement, contrapuntal combination, comes to the fore and takes on structural prominence.

The movement exhibits exact proportional symmetry, its two halves each comprising 112 measures.[23] The first half ends with a ritornello employing the outer segments (the antecedent and the epilogue) of the opening ritornello now transposed into the dominant, and the second half concludes with a complete statement of the opening ritornello at its original pitch. However, the *a'* segment of this central restatement of the ritornello is extended by a pedal point in which an original single echo is transformed and reiterated twice antiphonally between ripieno strings and solo violin playing double stops (see discussion on page 26). These additional four measures are later incorporated into the concluding statement of the ritornello. The movement thus rests firmly on three ritornello pillars that can be considered as dynamic rather than static, in that the final ritornello forms the sum of the two earlier ritornellos. (See Examples 5a, 5b, and 5c.)

Such a dynamic approach to form, in which there is what might be called continuous development, is typical of the rest of the movement. The proportional symmetry established is articulated on the formal level, as all three internal sections in the first

Hans-Günter Klein, *Der Einfluss der Vivaldischen Konzertform im Instrumentalwerk Johann Sebastian Bachs* (Strasbourg: Heitz, 1970), 45–46, to the ritornellos BWV 1056. There is indeed no real *Fortspinnung* in these ritornellos.

23. Klein, Der Einfluss der Vivaldischen Konzertform, 45–46.

Ex. 5a. BWV 1056[a]/3, mm. 1–24 (ritornello)

Ex. 5b. BWV 1056[a]/3, mm. 25–28

Ex. 5c. BWV 1056[a]/3, mm. 73–77

half are recapitulated in the same order in the second. However, Bach introduces some interesting variants. Only the opening solo *A* (mm. 113–36) represents an exact transposed repetition of its first statement at mm. 25–48 and thus provides a stable point of formal reference (important at the beginning of the second half), whereas the other three sections are significantly altered. The ritornello segment expected following this solo is replaced by a modulatory dialogue between violin 1 and solo parts based on an alternation of ritornello phrase *a* (mm. 137–48). The developmental character of this section is further reinforced by the imitative entries of the remaining ripieno parts based on the ritornello motive *x* in the version first stated in the continuo part at m. 4 (See *x'* in Example 5a).[24] It is therefore no coincidence that the sequence of five imitative entries, each one measure in length, is initiated by the bass. The concluding entry of *a* (m. 149ff) acts as a veritable *fausse reprise* (familiar from classical sonata form). It functions aurally both as the close of the dialogue and as the opening of the recapitulation of *aa'ba''* (mm. 149–65; cf. mm. 49–72). The transposed repetition of *B* is extended by a thematically free climactic passage comprising solo violin figuration over a dominant pedal point. This passage prepares for the reprise of the ritornello, the culmination of all preceding statements of it.

The cumulative nature of the second half argues against the repetition of *B* at the

24. P 234 offers no evidence for the theoretical possibility that this version with six sixteenth notes forms part of the transcription for solo cembalo alone.

lower octave (an intervention necessary if the movement is considered to have been originally scored for solo oboe) and in favor of its restatement at the octave above as a means of reinforcing the climactic buildup. (It is significant in this regard that A is transposed up a fifth at its restatement in the second half.) B, sounding a fifth lower at mm. 165ff rather than a fourth higher than the initial statement at mm. 73ff, appears out of context owing to the contrapuntal intensification by a new solo line and tense dominant pedal and to the increasing formal and musical tension characteristic of the second half of the movement.

The careful planning of the structure as a whole is clear from the developing relationship between solo and ripieno, a relationship in which the central dynamic at work is contrapuntal juxtaposition. Thus the initial solo theme, A, is at once answered canonically by violin 1 and the other three ripieno parts, which simultaneously introduce the simplified ritornello head motive x (violin 2 in the form y) in close imitation (Examples 5a and 5b). Something similar happens with the second solo theme (B) where the ripieno restates the head motive x unaltered over the space of two bars (also possibly conceived as a free interpretation of y), now including violin 1 (Example 5c).

The idea behind the increasing contrapuntal artifice in the statements of the ritornello after its initial statement at mm. 1–24 proves to be that of systematic accumulation. The solo extensions of the ritornello (with the exception of the development of a in mm. 137–49) are all based on a continuation and elaboration of the echo appendix of the antecedent (Example 5a). In mm. 55–62, the ripieno develops the forte/piano idea by repeating it at different pitch levels while figuration in the solo part is based on the head motive. As already noted, at mm. 98–104 and 202–8, the echo appears transformed as an antiphonal distribution of the motive between ripieno and solo repeated twice. Thus the contrapuntal writing in the ritornello segment at mm. 49–72 occurs only during the central extension and leaves the ritornello, as such, untouched. During the rest of the movement, these ritornello segments are increasingly "overgrown" by solo counterpoint, first for four (mm. 105–8), then for eight (mm. 155–62), and finally for twelve (mm. 209–20) measures. Indeed, the concluding statement of the ritornello forms the culmination of the piece; not only does it restate all ritornello segments and prolong a' with the extension first found in mm. 99–104, but it also enriches $ba''b'$ with solo counterpoint; that to the consequent ba'' has already been heard in mm. 157–63, and that to the epilogue phrase b' forms a canon with violin 1.[25] This

25. Note that the remaining three ripieno parts here are not altered, thus reinforcing the impression that this canonic combination had already been conceived by the time Bach composed the opening ritornello.

last contrapuntal coup, above all, confirms the status of BWV 1056/3 as a particularly sophisticated example of Bach's concerto composition.[26]

The first movement of BWV 1056 is the equal of the third in many respects and, moreover, forms its indisputable complement. Although cast in a similarly concise ritornello form, BWV 1056/1 exhibits rather different principles of construction. (See Figure 2.)

As in the third movement, Bach treats the ritornello (Example 6a) with consummate freedom. After its initial statement, it never recurs in its complete form. What is more, four of five ritornello segments (*a'*, *a"*, *b*, and *c*) recur only once. The ritornello head motive, *a*, on the other hand, furnishes the ritornello pillars necessary for a concerto structure and often does so in the most succinct way possible, as in the abbreviated statement in mm. 55–58 (notice in particular the omission of the upbeat to m. 57 in Example 6b) cut off by the soloist. Indeed, after the opening ritornello, the recurrences of ritornello segments take on an almost quotation-like character: they never achieve a fully independent status. The changed relationship between tutti and solo comes to the fore especially in a rather straightforward technique not employed in the last movement—that of rhythmic differentiation in which the ritornello is principally characterized by eighth and sixteenth notes, the solo by sixteenth triplets. The solo violin in fact spins out nonthematic triplet figuration almost continuously. (Ironically, the first solo is distinguished by strongly melodic elements, but these never recur in the ensuing solos as might be expected, and thus Bach's strategy seems to be to defeat the listener's expectations.) The only substantial repetition of a solo passage is to be found in the closing measures of solos 1 and 2 (mm. 31–34 and 67–70). The

---

26. In light of the contrapuntal writing here and elsewhere, especially between the solo violin and violin 1, it is likely that the ripieno was performed with one instrument per part, a performance practice for the version for solo cembalo now generally recognized as the most viable. Another related feature is that the basso continuo in that version was likely intended for one player per part, too, there played on a single eight-foot instrument. This is implied by the doublings of the continuo part in the cembalo bass part one octave higher in the first movement at m. 61 and in the third movement (mm. 36, 115–17, 139, 161–63, 168–69, and 176–82). With the addition of a sixteen-foot violone, the bass part in these passages would sound at three different octaves. Interesting in this regard are two passages in the first movement where Bach initially entered the cembalo bass part, first at m. 60 one octave higher (thus doubling the viola part at the unison) and then at m. 61 one octave lower (thus doubling the continuo part at the unison). He subsequently revised the two measures by exchanging the cembalo bass passages in each so that at m. 60 the cembalo bass part doubles the viola part at the lower octave and at m. 61, the continuo part at the upper octave. The addition of a sixteen-foot instrument to the continuo part at m. 61 would distort this symmetrical octave relationship. However, if one hypothesizes the existence at one time of a set of original parts along the lines of those for BWV 1055 (ST 127), one could imagine the same kind of greatly reduced violone part for BWV 1056 as that which exists for BWV 1055, in which the sixteen-foot instrument is silent in the passages mentioned, passages that, importantly, never include ritornello segments.

Figure 2. Formal analysis of BWV 1056/1

mm.	no.	ritornello	solo	tonal area*
1–20	20	*aa'ba"c*	solo plays epilogue (*a" c*)	**i** [→V/i→i]
21–34	14		solo 1	i→III
35–38	4	*a*		**III**
39–70	32	*a*	solo 2 with one fragmented ritornello interjection (*a*)	III→iv
71–78	8	*aa*		**iv / III**
79–82	4		solo 3	VI→V/i→
83–89	7	*ba*	solo plays *a*	V/i→i
90–108	19	(*a'/a*)	solo 4 with two 2–measure ritornello interjections (*a'a*)	**i**→V/i → i
109–16	8	*a"c*	solo-dominated	**i**

*main tonal areas in bold type

contrapuntal reworking of ritornello material and imitative/canonic accompaniment in the solo sections present in the last movement are both conspicuously absent here. Most revealing in this regard are the ritornello interpolations in solos 2 and 4, where a sustained note in the solo part interrupts chains of triplets (see Example 6b). The inherent danger of disconnectedness between the ritornello and solo is avoided by the deployment in the continuo part of a motive that functions as a kind of "quasi-ostinato" during almost the entire ritornello (*x* in Example 6a) and that, because of its frequent recurrence as accompanying material in the solo sections, plays a crucial unifying role. (See Examples 6a and 6b.)

As in the concluding movement, the reciprocal permeation of ripieno and solo is a central aim of the composer in the opening movement. This is achieved principally by giving the triplet figuration almost exclusively to the soloist. Solo figuration dominates even the last half of the ritornello, where the harmonies of the ripieno are embellished by triplet figuration (Example 5a). This unusual procedure sets the tone for the highly sophisticated structure of the rest of the movement, in particular that of its final phase (mm. 83–116), where all ritornello segments are recapitulated at their original pitch. But unusually, this reprise starts with the consequent phrase, *b*. Even more unexpected is the reentry of the soloist, who comes in, not as might be expected with the triplet continuation of the ripieno segment *a"* (which in the exposition follows upon *b*), but rather, with the statement of the head motive of the ritornello accompanied by the ripieno at m. 87.[27] What is more, this entry is reinterpreted in its continuation as a statement not of the consequent phrase *a"*, but rather of the antecedent phrase *a* with

27. See also Christian Berger, "J. S. Bachs Cembalokonzerte—Ein Beitrag zur Gattungsgeschichte des Klavierkonzertes im 18. Jahrhundert," *Archiv für Musikwissenschaft* 47 (1990): 211.

Ex. 6a. BWV 1056[a]/1, mm. 1–20 (ritornello)

Ex. 6b. BWV 1056[a]/1, mm. 55–58

its emphatic threefold repetition of the opening motive.[28] There can be little doubt that this entry functions aurally as the real reprise of the movement as a whole rather than simply as that at m. 83 of the consequent phrase, *b*.[29] This interpretation would seem to be confirmed by the fact that the tonic key, so emphatically reestablished by the soloist, is sustained for the rest of the movement, creating a reprise that occupies thirty measures, nearly a quarter of the movement as a whole. The soloistic nature of the opening of the reprise is further emphasized by its transposition to the upper octave and by the fact that here the solo part (except when doubling violin 1) is given sixteenth-note rather than triplet figuration for the first and only time.

The allocation to the solo violin of the formally crucial function of opening the reprise in BWV 1056/1 is symptomatic of the steadily increasing importance of the solo part at the expense of the ripieno, a process already begun in the final segment of the opening ritornello. Indeed, the solo has established its dominance by the time the reprise arrives, at which point the function of the ripieno has been reduced to mere accompaniment. In this respect, this passage corresponds closely to the final section of BWV 1056/3, even though the goal here is achieved through structural rather than contrapuntal means. This suggests that in the outer movements, Bach was aiming to create two contrasting manifestations of ritornello form within a single concerto and, in both cases, within as condensed a formal framework as possible. The result is to maximize individual refinement in the ripieno, where tonal structures are treated as autonomous factors played off one against the other in a consummate way.[30] The outer movements of BWV 1056 are clearly conceived as complementary, closely related compositions. Their compact dimensions are obviously in accord: their durations are virtually the same after equalization of the fastest note values (twelve sixteenth-note triplets for each $\frac{2}{4}$ measure correspond with twelve sixteenth notes for two $\frac{3}{8}$ measures, yielding the proportion 29:28).

Even more important is the close relation between their tonal structures. (See Figure 3.)

Figure 3. Main tonal areas of BWV 1056/1,3

BWV 1056/1: i – III – iv – III – i	[ritornello: i – V/i – i]
BWV 1056/3: i – III – v – iv – i	[ritornello: i – III – i]

28. This interpretation might have consequences for a textual detail: the triplet at m. 89 should have the "Neapolitan" lowered auxiliary of m. 3 (it was probably simply forgotten in P 234).

29. This interpretation differs significantly from the analysis of Hans-Günter Klein, who considers only the last eight measures, mm. 109ff, as such (*Der Einfluß der Vivaldischen Konzertform*, 68).

30. On this, see Laurence Dreyfus, "J. S. Bach's Concerto Ritornellos and the Question of Invention," *Musical Quarterly* 71 (1985): 327–58.

After the opening statement of the ritornello in the tonic, both movements proceed to the mediant and establish the subdominant scale degree later. In the first movement this subdominant region is placed centrally and is followed by yet another statement in the mediant, thus setting up a strictly symmetrical tonal plan with the reprise in the tonic. The last movement, on the other hand, establishes the dominant as its central tonality, a fact that may be explained by its origins as a stylized dance movement (see page 51). It is striking that the scale degree "missing" as a center in the overall tonal plan of one movement plays, by contrast, a crucial role in the main ritornello of the other. Thus the consequent phrase in the ritornello of the opening movement is in the dominant, whereas the closing movement is in the mediant. These strict tonal parallels serve as a final argument for Bach's having conceived the two outer movements as an inextricably interrelated, complementary pair.

By analogy, there is a strong interconnection between the ritornellos themselves. The most striking feature they have in common is the melodic shape of the first consequent phrase of both structures (mm. 9ff). (See Examples 7a, 7b, and 7c.)

Further, they are both built up from four-measure units, imparting to them an unusually strict periodicity, and they both include echo writing. In the ritornello of the opening movement, the echo effect (mm. 4, 8) takes the form of an unaccompanied repetition by the soloist of a mordent-like motive from the ripieno. In the ritornello of the closing movement, the echo is stated in the ripieno itself (mm. 8 and 16) and subsequently, taken over by the soloist, is recast as a dialogue between tutti and solo. In addition, one should note the prominence of on-beat appoggiaturas harmonized by secondary dominant harmonies in the solo sections of both movements (in the opening movement at mm. 32 and 68 and in the closing movement at mm. 38/40 and 126/128), as well as the conspicuous use of cadenza-like solo figuration over a ripieno dominant pedal climactically just before the final ritornello (in the opening movement at mm. 96–101 and in the closing movement at mm. 183–96). Like the dynamic, through-composed structure of these movements, this latter feature is certainly Vivaldian.[31]

From these analytical observations, two conclusions can be drawn. First, the similarities in the formal planning of the outer movements confirm that they originate from a common *Urform* and thus must both share the same original solo instrument. Second, formally and compositionally they are without a doubt among Bach's most

---

31. Also ultimately derivative of Vivaldi is the strict division in BWV 1056/1 between thematic ritornello material and nonthematic solo episodes. A clear example from Vivaldi's concerto oeuvre is the Concerto for Violin, Strings, and Continuo in G Major, op. 3 no. 3 (transcribed by Bach for solo cembalo as BWV 978). That this work may well have something to do with the concept of BWV 1056 is also suggested by a feature in the closing tutti of its concluding movement. The strong chordal strokes (mm. 137ff) here are rhythmically identical to those that occur at the same point structurally in Bach's concerto.

Ex. 7a. BWV 1056[a]/1, mm. 9–12/BWV 1056(a)/3, mm. 9–12, violin 1

Ex. 7b. BWV 1056[a]/1, mm. 31–32/BWV 1056(a)/3,
mm. 37–38, violino concertato and continuo]

Ex. 7c. BWV 1056[a]/3, mm. 37–38

sophisticated concerto movements. Because of this sophistication and because it evidently constitutes his shortest essay in the concerto genre, the Violin Concerto in G minor (BWV 1056[a]) must claim a special position in the composer's oeuvre.

The Lost Middle Movement: A Hypothesis

Werner Breig's study of P 234[32] has demonstrated that the concertos were not transcribed in the order in which they appear in the autograph. Rather, the transcription of

---

32. A notable exception is the Concerto for Flute, Violin, Cembalo, Strings, and Continuo in A Minor (BWV 1044), but the models for its three movements—the A-Minor Prelude and Fugue (BWV 894) and the "Adagio e dolce" second movement of the third Organ Sonata (BWV 527)—do not originate in Bach's concerto oeuvre.

the last two, BWV 1058 and 1059, must have taken place before that of BWV 1052–57.[33] Physically, the foliation of P 234 reflects this sequence of transcription, in that the fascicle containing BWV 1058 and 1059 may have been bound at a later point after the other works had been entered. Breig observes that the two concertos in the initial layer demonstrate two very different approaches to the problem of transforming a concerto for solo melody instrument into a concerto for solo cembalo.[34] On the one hand, BWV 1058 remains closer to its model, the A-Minor Violin Concerto (BWV 1041), than do any other of the concertos, whereas BWV 1059 involves a far-reaching intervention affecting the very substance of its model, the first movement of the putative D-minor oboe concerto BWV 1059[a], right from the beginning of the opening ritornello. It was the impracticality of continuing this radical transcription method without parallel in BWV 1052–58 that induced Bach to give up work on BWV 1059 after the opening ritornello.[35] Thus BWV 1058–59 mark the initial, still rather experimental stage in the development of transcription for solo cembalo, perhaps serving as a "trial balloon" for a planned collection of six concertos subsequently realized in BWV 1052–57.[36] When Bach arrived at the point of arranging the G-Minor Violin Concerto (the fifth piece of the set), he decided not to use its original slow movement. Instead, he took the middle movement from the D-minor oboe concerto, which he had put aside after the transcription of its opening page, and thus was still available for use.[37] In the process, it seems that the slow movement of the violin concerto was lost.

However, it is possible that the rejected slow movement for BWV 1056 has not completely vanished and that a fragment remains in the form of a torso, BWV Anh. I 2, an incipit Bach jotted on the back page of the autograph score of the motet *Der Geist hilft unser Schwachheit auf* (BWV 226 [P 36/1]) with the heading "Concerto Do-

---

33. See Werner Breig, "Zum Kompositionsprozeß in Bachs Cembalokonzerte," in *Johann Sebastian Bachs Spätwerk und dessen Umfeld—Perspektiven and Probleme. Bericht über das wissenschaftliche Symposium anläßlich des 61. Bachfestes der neuen Bachgesellschaft, Duisburg, 28.-30. Mai 1986*, ed. Christoph Wolff (Kassel: Bärenreiter, 1988), 44–47, and NBA VII/4, KB, 19–20.

34. Breig, "Zum Kompositionsprozeß in Bachs Cembalokonzerte," 46.

35. See Werner Breig, "Bachs Cembalokonzert-Fragment in d-moll (BWV 1059)," BJ 65 (1979): 29–36.

36. BWV 1058 was probably bound later to appear after BWV 1052–57, so as to form some sort of appendix to the "opus." The fragment BWV 1059 was not lost, for the sole reason that it was notated on the verso side of the last page of BWV 1058. It was almost certainly not Bach's intention "to follow up these six concertos by another set of six," as suggested in Georg von Dadelsen, "Bemerkungen zu Bachs Cembalokonzerte," in *Bericht über die Wissenschaftliche Konferenz zum V. Internationalen Bach-Fest der DDR Leipzig 28.-31. März 1985*, ed. Winfried Hoffmann and Armin Schneiderheinze (Leipzig: Deutscher Verlag für Musik, 1987), 238.

37. This observation can be taken as another argument in favor of Breig's hypothesis for the relative chronology of the contents of P 234 (see note 33).

menica 19 post Trinitatis à 4 Voci. 1 Violino Conc: 2 Violini / Viole e Cont. di Bach."[38] Work on this cantata seems to have been interrupted by the urgent need to produce a motet for the funeral of the rector of the Thomaskirche, Johann Heinrich Ernesti, on October 20, 1729.[39] The planned cantata thus would seem to have been intended for the ensuing Sunday, October 23, the Nineteenth Sunday after Trinity.[40]

Although the six-measure fragment carries neither tempo indication nor genre designation, it can be identified as an instrumental sinfonia.[41] Moreover, it is clearly identifiable as a siciliano, a slow movement. It cannot be the introductory ritornello to an aria, for two reasons. First, as a rule Bach notates his (solo) vocal parts directly above the lowest, continuo staff, below the other instrumental parts, but here the solo part is notated on the highest staff. Second, and even more important, this upper part is not notated in the soprano clef but rather in the treble clef, used by Bach only, as far as I am aware, for notating instrumental parts. Thus, this empty staff must have been destined for the "Violino Conc:" of the title. Its specification here serves as another clear indicator pointing to a sinfonia for solo violin, as Bach never included the modifier *solo* in his cantata titles when the instrument functions merely as an obbligato instrument in an aria—not even in the autograph score of a cantata such as *Erfreute Zeit im neuen Bunde* (BWV 83), which is dominated by virtuosic writing for solo violin throughout (although it includes no sinfonia).[42]

38. See the facsimile, *Johann Sebastian Bach: Der Geist hilft unser Schwachheit auf, Motette* BWV 226, ed. Konrad Ameln (Kassel: Bärenreiter, 1964).

39. See Martin Geck, "Zur Datierung, Verwendung and Aufführungspraxis von Bachs Motetten," in *Bach-Studien* 5, ed. Rudolf Eller and Hans-Joachim Schulze (Leipzig: Deutscher Verlag für Musik, 1975), 63–64.

40. Martin Geck observes that in the third movement of the motet *Der Geist hilft unsrer Schwachheit auf* (BWV 226), the four-part vocal fugue "Der aber die Herzen forschet," there are many corrections in the text but hardly any in the music, and he notes that there is a certain incongruity between music and text, all of which clearly points to a parody (Geck, "Zur Datierung, Verwendung and Aufführungspraxis," 65). Because this fugue, like the rest of the motet, is in the same key as the sinfonia fragment, B♭ major, one wonders whether it was not meant to form part of the aborted cantata in the same key originally intended to follow the sinfonia. A similar constellation, a sinfonia followed by a four-part "Allabreve" fugue, opens the cantata *Wir danken dir, Gott, wir danken dir* (BWV 29) of 1731. Moreover, both fugues are thematically related. If this hypothesis is correct, then the key of BWV 226 was predetermined by that of the aborted cantata.

41. On this, see also Klaus Häfner, "Der Picander-Jahrgang," BJ 61 (1975): 99–100.

42. See Matthias Wendt and Uwe Wolf, eds., NBA I/28.1 (*Kantaten zu Marienfesten I*), KB, 11. On BWV 83 and its exceptional use of a solo violin, see Pieter Dirksen, "Die Kantate *Erfreute Zeit im neuen Bunde* BWV 83 und die Rolle der Violine in Bachs erstem Leipziger Jahrgang," in *Bachs erster Leipziger Kantatenjahrgang. Dortmunder Bach-Forschungen* 4, ed. Martin Geck and Siegfried Oechsle (Witten: Klangfarben-Verlag, 2002), 135–56.

Plate 1. J. S. Bach, BWV Anh. I 2 (Berlin, Staatsbibliothek zu Berlin, Mus. ms. P 36/1, fol. 8v [= p. 18]). (Reproduced with the permission of the Staatsbibliothek zu Berlin—Preussischer Kulturbesitz)

That the fragment, BWV Anh. I 2, represents a new composition would seem to be a remote possibility given that newly composed instrumental movements are notably absent in the surviving cantatas of Bach's Leipzig period; nearly all such extant pieces appear to be transcriptions.[43] BWV Anh. I 2 fits better in the context of an important tendency in Bach's cantata compositions during the years 1726–29, when he sought to recycle a large number of extant concerto movements in otherwise newly composed cantatas.[44] This all leads to the conclusion that BWV Anh. I 2 represents the remains of the middle movement of a lost violin concerto in G minor that, considering the rather narrow boundaries of Bach's concerto oeuvre as a whole, could belong to no other work but the violin concerto whose outer movements have been arranged as BWV 1056/1,3. Its identification as a slow concerto movement is further supported by a comparison with the siciliana BWV 1053/2, preserved in what is likely its original form and at its original pitch in the cantata *Gott allein soll mein Herze haben* (BWV 169). In particular, the melodic shape of the opening and the offbeat bass pattern are of note. (See Examples 8a, 8b, and 8c.)

In two respects, BWV Anh. I 2 is closely related conceptually to the "Sinfonia" BWV 156/1, which probably dates to the same year, 1729.[45] First, both pieces are the only slow concerto movements adapted subsequently as introductory sinfonias to cantatas. Second, within the corpus of church cantatas, they are the only movements in which the original solo melody part has not been transcribed for obbligato organ. Perhaps the link between these two sinfonias, or rather between the two small-scale concertos to which they originally belonged, BWV 1056[a] and 1059[a],[46] served as a further incentive for Bach to combine BWV 156/1 with the outer movements of the violin concerto nine years later in his transcription for solo cembalo.[47]

Reinmar Emans has advanced the hypothesis that BWV 156 was composed not,

43. The only exceptions are the instrumental chorale arrangement concluding Bach's first Leipzig cantata, *Die Elenden sollen essen* (BWV 75), and the "Sinfonia" (BWV 248/10), which opens the second part of the Christmas Oratorio.

44. See the overview in Alfred Dürr, *Die Kantaten von Johann Sebastian Bach* (Kassel: Bärenreiter, 1971), 55.

45. Alfred Dürr, *Zur Chronologie der Leipziger Vokalwerke J. S. Bachs* (Kassel: Bärenreiter, 1976), 98.

46. As the text of cantata BWV 156 belongs to the "Picander" Jahrgang, the inner connection of its sinfonia with BWV Anh. I 2 may be seen as a further argument to associate the planned cantata for the Nineteenth Sunday after Trinity with the corresponding text from this Jahrgang, "Gott, du Richter der Gedanken." See also Klaus Häfner, "Der Picander-Jahrgang," 100. It should be noted, however, that the declamation of the text does not accord with the upbeat fugue subject of BWV 226/3 tentatively connected with BWV Anh. I 2 (see note 40).

47. Were these two concertos preserved together by Bach in the same manuscript or in the same wrapper?

Ex. 8a. BWV Anh. I 2, mm. 1–4, *ante correcturam*

Ex. 8b. BWV Anh. I 2, mm. 2–4, *post correcturam*

Ex. 8c. BWV 169/5 (= 1053[a]/2), mm. 1–2

as usually assumed, in 1729 but much earlier, in the Weimar period.[48] His principal argument is based on the style of the sinfonia, which he argues is not typical for the Leipzig period but rather points to Weimar. He thus entertains the possibility that BWV 156/1 was composed specially for the cantata, of which an early version could then be dated to the Weimar period. However, there are several objections to this hypothesis. Emans's observation that "the use of a solo oboe is more characteristic of the Weimar than of the Leipzig cantatas"[49] is problematic in that only two such Weimar cantata sinfonias are extant—BWV 12/1 and BWV 21/1. Moreover, these movements are stylistically rather different from BWV 156/1. The "archaic" five-part string accompaniment with two violas of BWV 12/1, and the fact that BWV 21/1 is not an accompanied solo but rather a trio sonata movement for oboe, violin, and continuo, distinguishes these Weimar sinfonias chronologically from BWV 156/1. The latter movement, with its simple, completely homophonic four-part string accompaniment and unusually transparent periodicity clearly belongs to a later stage of Bach's stylistic development.

Because the text of BWV 156 was published in 1728 in a collection by Picander,[50] the performance of the cantata (preserved only in a late copy) has been dated to 1729. Emans's hypothesis of an early dating for BWV 156/1 forced him to argue that Picander's text was a parody of an early Weimar version of the cantata, a reconstruction of the work's source history, which even he admits is not obvious.[51] In the face of such uncertainty retaining 1729 as the date of composition of the cantata would seem preferable to Emans's early dating. Identifying BWV Anh. I 2 as the slow movement of BWV 1056[a], and its intentional reuse unaltered as a cantata sinfonia, moreover, frees BWV 156/1 from its previously isolated position in Bach's oeuvre.[52]

---

48. "Überlegungen zu den Konzert- und Instrumentalsätzen in Johann Sebastian Bachs Kantaten," in *Beiträge zur Geschichte des Konzertes—Festschrift Siegfried Kross zum 60. Geburtstag*, ed. Reinmar Emans and Matthias Wendt (Bonn: Schröder, 1990), 47–49.

49. Emans, "Überlegungen zu den Konzert- und Instrumentalsätzen," 47.

50. In his *Cantaten auf die Sonn- und Fest-Tage durch das gantze Jahr* (Leipzig, 1728).

51. "Wenngleich der Text in den Arien gut—man ist gerade geneigt zu sagen: zu gut—zur Musik paßt, müßte eine Spezialstudie zu klären versuchen, ob es sich dennoch (oder gerade darum?) um eine Parodie handeln könnte. Ausgeschlossen jedenfalls ist dies nicht." Emans, "Überlegungen zu den Konzert- und Instrumentalsätzen," 48.

52. It should also be noted that the only cantata for which we have concrete evidence of a performance in 1729, *Ich liebe den Höchsten von ganzem Gemüte* (BWV 174), includes a sinfonia that, like BWV 156/1 and BWV Anh. I 2, makes no use of obbligato organ and preserves intact the original instrumentation. BWV 174/1 is an arrangement of the first movement of the Third Brandenburg Concerto (BWV 1048), augmented by horns and oboes.

One can only speculate on Bach's motives for deciding to omit the original slow movement of BWV 1056[a] in favor of one culled from a different concerto. However, a particular feature of the autograph fragment may offer a clue. There are a number of clearly visible corrections[53] that, although they appear at first sight to point to a composing score, on closer scrutiny are revealed to constitute alterations of an extant movement. The corrections led to a harmonic enrichment of a more straightforward, but in itself complete, four-part composition. Perhaps this critique of his own work foreshadowed his rejection of it nine years later as the slow movement of BWV 1056.

Bach's decision may also have been occasioned by a preference on his part for a woodwind piece as the slow movement to BWV 1056. Here a comparison of the middle movements of the violin concertos BWV 1041, 1042, and 1052a with those of the oboe concertos BWV 1053[a], 1055[a], and 1059[a] is instructive. One of the principal differences is that the melodies for solo violin tend toward long-held notes much more than do those for solo oboe. Although as a rule, the longest note values in the cantilenas for oboe have a duration of a (dotted) quarter note and at most take up half a measure, long-held notes of a full measure's duration are widespread in the violin cantilenas. The solo melody of the Adagio (BWV 1042/2), for example, enters on a note held for over two full measures. In the arrangement for harpsichord BWV 1054/2, Bach attempts to alleviate the problem of the harpsichord's inability to sustain notes by adding a very unusual ornament, namely a held mordent (François Couperin's *pincé continu*).[54] It is therefore likely that such held notes were a prominent feature in BWV 1056[a]/2, too, a good reason for Bach not to include it in his transcription for solo cembalo.

Some speculation concerning the formal features of the B♭-major movement is possible. Considering that it would originally have been framed by two of Bach's shortest concerto movements, one can be fairly certain that it was structured as a straightforward ABA movement in which two identical ritornellos, for the greater part paralleling the fragment BWV Anh. I 2 (it seems to lack only two measures of cadential material and therefore must originally have been eight measures long), framed a single longer solo, now lost. The two other siciliano slow movements of concertos, BWV 1053/2 and

53. See Robert L. Marshall, *The Compositional Process of J. S. Bach* (Princeton, N.J.: Princeton University Press, 1972), 2:148; BC A 147.

54. François Couperin, "Explication des Agrémens et des Signes," in *Pièces de Clavecin—Premier Livre* (Paris, 1713). The ornament appears only once elsewhere in Bach's oeuvre, in the second half of the gigue from the sixth English Suite (BWV 811), which consists of a very sophisticated inversion of the first half of the piece (see Ulrich Siegele, "Die musiktheoretische Lehre einer Bachschen Gigue," *Archiv für Musikwissenschaft* 17 (1960): 152–67), in which, as the ultimate consequence of the process of inversion, the sustained upper-note trills of the first half are inverted, as well. As such, its use here must be considered exceptional.

1055/2, confirm this. Although they both are part of longer concertos and are thus more substantial structures than BWV 1056[a]/2 would have been, they both adopt the same simple tripartite structure proposed here. Thus the lost siciliano for solo violin was undoubtedly not only formally similar to those for oboe but must also have been shorter than these two movements (35 and 39 measures in $\frac{12}{8}$ meter, respectively).

Toward a Dating

Having confirmed that the two outer movements of BWV 1056 belong to a common *Urform* and tentatively identified its original slow movement, the outlines of Bach's G-Minor Violin Concerto are once again clearly discernible. Although the fragmentary nature of the middle movement prevents a complete reconstruction and thus a workable performing version of the work, its clear identity as a siciliano may have important chronological ramifications. But apart from this, several stylistic features of the outer movements provide firm clues for arriving at a chronology of the concerto as a whole.

There has been a general tendency to place the G-Minor Concerto (that is, its outer movements) rather early in Bach's output. Wilfried Fischer does so because in his view the work is "not as developed as the extant violin concertos,"[55] whereas Hans-Joachim Schulze takes the composite nature of the transcription for solo cembalo, BWV 1056, and the implied critical attitude of Bach pointing to two different concertos as indicative of a relatively early dating.[56]

Although my analysis refutes any implication of a lack of compositional sophistication, the latter argument must be taken more seriously, as all of those concertos in which Bach altered the structure in one way or another (BWV 1046a, 1050a, 1052a) seem to date back to the Weimar period.[57] But all of these three works exhibit experimental formal and/or compositional traits that are notably absent in BWV 1056. The

55. NBA VII/7, KB, 83f Klein (*Der Einfluss der Vivaldischen Konzertform*, 49) concurs with this view and goes even further by suggesting that BWV 1056[a] "als eines der ersten Konzerte Bachs angesehen wird und vielleicht sogar schon in Weimar entstanden ist."

56. Hans-Joachim Schulze, "Nachwort" in *Joh. Seb. Bach: Konzert f-moll für Cembalo und Streichorchester* BWV 1056 (Leipzig: Peters, 1977); Hans-Joachim Schulze, "Johann Sebastian Bachs Konzerte—Fragen der Überlieferung und Chronologie," in *Beiträge zum Konzertschaffen Johann Sebastian Bachs*, *Bach-Studien* 6, ed. Peter Ansehl, Karl Heller, and Hans-Joachim Schulze (Leipzig: Breitkopf and Härtel, 1981), 16.

57. On BWV 1046a, see Schulze, "Bachs Konzerte—Fragen der Überlieferung and Chronologie," 16–18; on BWV 1050a (Summer, 1717?), see Pieter Dirksen, "The Background to Bach's Fifth Brandenburg Concerto," in *The Harpsichord and Its Repertoire*, ed. Pieter Dirksen (Utrecht: STIMU, 1992), 157–85; on BWV 1052a, see Werner Breig, "Bachs Violinkonzert in d-moll—Studien zu seiner Gestalt und seiner Entstehungsgeschichte," BJ 62 (1976): 7–34.

latter work clearly belongs to a much later stage of Bach's compositional development. The view that the outer movements of BWV 1056 are "less developed"[58] has obviously been occasioned more by their restricted length than by any formal or thematic considerations, the result of a mindset encountered rather often in Bach studies than in other areas of musicological research.[59] On the contrary, the small scale of these movements clearly has nothing to do with an early stage of Bach's concerto composition. Rather, the reverse seems to be true.

The dating of the fragment, BWV Anh. I 2, establishes a *terminus ante quem* of 1729 for the G-Minor Concerto as a whole. However, as this fragment belongs to a series of Leipzig cantata sinfonias from the years 1725–31, all of which have their origins for the most part in preexistent concertos that go back to the pre-Leipzig period,[60] this *terminus ante quem* can probably be shifted even further back in time to 1723. Because, in my view, a Weimar origin can be excluded, it seems probable that this work originated in Köthen. This is also suggested by the identity of BWV Anh. I 2 as a siciliano, assuming that it is indeed the slow movement of BWV 1056[a]. There are no traces of Bach's use of the siciliano before the Köthen period, and it appears regularly only in the Leipzig cantatas.[61] Only a single example of a movement titled "Siciliano" can definitely be dated to the Köthen period—the third movement of the Sonata for Solo Violin in G Minor (BWV 1001) of 1720. Of the undated works besides the G-Minor Concerto that incorporate siciliano movements, only two, the Concerto for Oboe d'Amore in A major (BWV 1055[a]) and the cantata fragment BWV 184a can be dated with any certainty to the Köthen period.[62]

58. Schulze, "Nachwort," in *Joh. Seb. Bach: Konzert f-moll*.

59. For a particularly striking example, see Pieter Dirksen, "Bachs 'Acht Choralfughetten'—Ein unbeachtetes Leipziger Sammelwerk?" in *Bach in Leipzig—Bach und Leipzig. Bach-Konferenz Leipzig 2000. Leipziger Beiträge zur Bachforschung 5*, ed. Ulrich Leisinger (Hildesheim: Georg Olms Verlag, 2002), 155–82.

60. A possible exception is BWV 1053[a]; see Gregory Butler, "J. S. Bach's Reception of the Mature Concertos of Tomaso Albinoni," in *Bach Studies 2*, ed. Daniel Melamed (Cambridge: Cambridge University Press, 1995), 20–46.

61. Doris Fincke-Hecklinger, *Tanzcharaktere in Johann Sebastian Bachs Vokalmusik* (Trossingen: Hohner-Verlag, 1970), 81–88. See also Reinhard Wiesend, "'Erbarme dich', alla Siciliana," in *Bach und die Italienische Musik. Centro Tedesco di Studi Veneziani—Quaderni 36*, ed. Wolfgang Osthoff and Reinhard Wiesend (Venice: Centro Tedesco di Studi Veneziani, 1988), 19–41.

62. The Sonata for Violin and Cembalo in C Minor (BWV 1017), the Concerto for Two Cembali in C Major (BWV 1061a), as well as BWV 1053(a), all of which include siciliano movements, may have originated in Leipzig rather than in Köthen. On BWV 1017, see Hans-Joachim Schulze, *Studien zur Bach-Überlieferung im 18. Jahrhundert* (Leipzig and Dresden: Peters, 1984), 110–19; on BWV 1061a, see Christoph Wolff, "Bach's Leipzig Chamber Music," in Wolff, *Bach: Essays on His Life and Music*

The outer movements of the G-Minor Concerto have some unusual features in common with a small clutch of concertos, suggesting that they date from the same period. In particular, not only does BWV 1055 exhibit the same strict periodic structure throughout, but its first movement observes the same clear differentiation between ritornello and solo material, and in its concluding movement, one notes the same close interweaving of solo and ritornello material. Even more suggestive of their occupying together a separate branch of Bach's concerto oeuvre is the unique structure of the four ritornellos of their outer movements. Hans-Günther Klein observes that they do not adhere to the usual format, *Vordersatz–Fortspinnung–Epilog*. Rather, the central part is replaced by a nonsequential *Nachsatz* forming a full pendant to the *Vordersatz*.[63] (I have used the English equivalents "antecedent–consequent–epilogue" for the resulting tripartite structure in the analysis offered here.) This ritornello structure, which could perhaps be referred to as a *Liedtypus*[64] enlarged by a secondary consequent (the epilogue) is not encountered again in Bach's concerto oeuvre.

On the other hand, some important differences between the two concertos should be noted. Although the ritornellos of the outer movements of BWV 1055 restrict themselves for the most part to the tonic and the dominant, their counterparts in BWV 1056 are more adventurous. Correspondingly, within the bounds of a similarly balanced periodic structure, the outer movements of BWV 1056 are formally more sophisticated than those of BWV 1055. Indeed, there is no hint of a gradually dissolving ritornello form in the A-major concerto, suggesting that BWV 1056[a] is a work from the late Köthen period. The only other work whose ritornello displays a similar form is that of the first movement of the Concerto for Two Violins, Strings, and Continuo in D Minor (BWV 1043), a work now generally accepted to date from the Leipzig period. In the opening movements of these two concertos, moreover, the solo material remains entirely separate from the tutti material, whereas the use of two different solo themes, the canonic writing, and the contrapuntal undercurrent throughout BWV 1056/3 link it with both outer movements of BWV 1043. Similarly, the closing movement of BWV 1043 relates to BWV 1056/1 in highlighting the independent participation of the soloist(s) right from the opening ritornello, a feature otherwise encountered only in BWV 1042/1 and 1060/1.

(Cambridge, Mass.: Harvard University Press, 1993), 169, and Karl Heller, "Zur Stellung des Concerto C-Dur für zwei Cembali BWV 1061 in Bachs Konzert-Oeuvre," in *Bericht über die Wissenschaftliche Konferenz zum V. Internationalen Bach-Fest 1985*, ed. Winfried Hoffmann and Armin Schneiderheinze (Leipzig: Deutscher Verlag für Musik, 1987), 249–50; on BWV 1053[a], see Butler, "J. S. Bach's Reception of the Mature Concertos of Tomaso Albinoni," 39–44.

63. Klein, *Der Einfluss der Vivaldischen Konzertform*, 45–46.

64. On this type, see Hio-Ihm Lee, *Die Form der Ritornelle bei Johann Sebastian Bach* (Pfaffenweiler: Centaurus Verlagsgesellschaft, 1993), 123–26.

The latter piece, the C-Minor Concerto for Oboe and Violin (BWV 1060[a]), is a third work bearing a close resemblance to BWV 1056. The closely related solo echoes in the ritornellos of the opening movements of both pieces have already been noted, but the kinship between these two ritornellos goes even further. In both instances, the antecedent consists of two four-measure phrases in which the second phrase forms a transposed repeat of the first. In BWV 1060/1, the transposition of the second phrase down by step differs from that to the subdominant in BWV 1056/1. However, the repeat of the complete antecedent in the latter movement (mm. 71–78) is also transposed down by step, from iv to III. A feature of both outer movements of BWV 1056 (and therefore particularly characteristic for the piece as a whole) is the virtuosic solo figuration over a dominant pedal point harmonized by the full ripieno just before the closing statement of the ritornello. The only other example in Bach's oeuvre is to be found in the closing movement of BWV 1060 (mm. 125–34). Similarly, the bipartite structure of BWV 1056/3 with two similarly structured halves is otherwise to be found only in BWV 1060/1, although there, it is without the same strict proportional symmetry.[65]

Unfortunately for our purposes, establishing a chronology for these two concertos that stand perhaps the closest to the G-Minor Concerto is problematic, in that their original versions, BWV 1055[a] and BWV 1060[a], have also been lost. However, the remaining work, the Concerto for Two Violins, Strings, and Continuo in D Minor (BWV 1043), may provide a clue to their dating. This concerto is no longer held to be a Köthen composition but was probably composed around 1730 or slightly later.[66] The characteristics it shares with the G-Minor Concerto may therefore suggest a dating for BWV 1056 to Bach's Leipzig period. In addition, the fact that in 1720 the solo melody instrument in BWV 1055[a], the oboe d'amore, was only just beginning to make its appearance at German courts[67] may place this work chronologically well into the 1720s. According to Walther's lexicon, the instrument was introduced around 1720[68] and was apparently a Leipzig specialty.[69] Accordingly, it never appears in Bach's pre-Leipzig cantatas and was used for the first time, apparently at the

---

65. Klein, Der Einfluß der Vivaldischen Konzertform, 68–69.

66. See Wolff, "Bach's Leipzig Chamber Music," 234–47. The theory of a trio sonata *Urfassung* without ripieno for BWV 1043 that supposedly originated in Köthen (Rampe and Sackmann, BOM, 108–10) is scarcely tenable; both the writing and the thematic structure argue strongly against it. Indeed structurally, this concerto often *resembles* a trio sonata, but this merely reflects an advanced, if not final, stage in Bach's shift in emphasis away from ritornello to soloist(s) clearly visible in BWV 1056[a].

67. On the identification of oboe d'amore as the solo melody instrument for BWV 1055a, see note 2.

68. Johann Gottfried Walther, "Hautbois d'Amour," in *Musicalisches Lexicon* (Leipzig, 1732), 304.

69. Bruce Haynes, "Oboe d'amore," in BOM, 284–85.

last minute,[70] in the cantata *Du wahrer Gott und Davids Sohn* (BWV 23), the Leipzig *Probestück* of February 1723. Werner Breig thus rightly concludes that "one can with some certainty situate the Concerto for Oboe d'amore in Bach's concerto oeuvre of the late Coethen period."[71] From this perspective, BWV 1056[a], clearly composed later, might then be dated toward the very end of that period. One of the principal stylistic grounds on which Breig's argument for a relatively late chronology of BWV 1055[a] is based, a "move towards periodicity" in his late concerto oeuvre,[72] has been further substantiated by Wolfgang Hirschmann,[73] who points in particular to four works by Bach—BWV 1055[a], BWV 1056[a], BWV 1060[a], as well as the Italian Concerto (BWV 971). The first three works are closely related, as we have seen, whereas BWV 971 is a Leipzig work, probably from the same final stage of Bach's concerto composition as BWV 1043, that is, around 1730. That BWV 1056[a] exemplifies this trend is clear from the four-measure periods of its ritornello and the predominance of four-measure periods and their multiples in the outer movements. Hirschmann also suggests the music of Telemann as an influence on this aspect of Bach's concerto composition. Because this influence became a factor only after around 1719, an even later *terminus post quem* may have to be posited for Bach's use of this technique.

That the concluding movement of BWV 1056 is a highly stylized dance movement is confirmed by its division into two equal halves with a prominent cadence in the dominant precisely at the midpoint, a feature routinely encountered in suite movements but unusual in a concerto.[74] The melodic and harmonic style of this movement

---

70. See Christoph Wolff, "Bach's Audition for the St. Thomas Cantorate: The Cantata 'Du wahrer Gott and Davids Sohn,'" in Christoph Wolff, *Bach: Essays on His Life and Music* (Cambridge, Mass.: Harvard University Press, 1993), 134.

71. Werner Breig, "Zur Chronologie von Johann Sebastian Bachs Konzertschaffen—Versuch eines neuen Zugangs," in *Archiv für Musikwissenschaft* 40 (1983): 101. See also NBA VII/7, KB, 65; Hans-Joachim Schulze, "Johann Sebastian Bachs Konzerte—Fragen der Überlieferung and Chronologie," 13–15.

72. In Breig, "Zur Chronologie von Bachs Konzertschaffen," 80–83 and 98–101. See also Werner Breig, "Periodenbau in Bachs Konzerte," in *Beiträge zum Konzertschaffen Johann Sebastian Bachs. Bach-Studien 6*, ed. Peter Ansehl, Karl Heller, and Hans-Joachim Schulze (Leipzig: Breitkopf und Härtel, 1981), 37–38.

73. Wolfgang Hirschmann, "Eklektischer Imitationsbegriff und konzertantes Gestalten bei Telemann und Bach," in BOW, 314–15. *Bachs Orchesterwerke*. Dortmunder Bach-Forschungen 1, ed. Martin Geck and Werner Breig (Witten: Klangfarben-Verlag, 1997). On the influence of Telemann's concertos on Bach, see also Ian Payne, "Telemann's Musical Style, c. 1709–c. 1730 and J. S. Bach: The Evidence of Borrowing," *Bach* 30 (1999): 42–64.

74. By nature, this AB form is fundamentally different from the AB form recognized by Gregory

in $\frac{3}{8}$ meter and its strict four-measure periodic structure point to the passepied (as do the on-beat sixteenths and the syncopations), all features that occur in abundance in the solo part, as well.[75] The rather passionate, agitated manner of the movement can also be linked to this dance type, notable, according to Mattheson, for its "disquiet and inconstancy."[76] Passepieds are rare in Bach's music; movements titled "Passepied" all date from the 1720s and 1730s.[77] Of particular interest in this regard is the occurrence of another stylized passepied as the concluding movement of the Concerto for Violin, Strings, and Continuo in E Major (BWV 1042) (here cast in the mold of a strict rondo), as it has recently been convincingly redated to the mid-1720s.[78] The inclusion of solo insertions in the opening ritornello of its first movement provides further evidence that it belongs to a late contingent of Bach's concerto compositions which stem from the late Köthen/early Leipzig period between BWV 1055[a], BWV 1060[a], BWV 1056[a] as a group and BWV 1053[a]. A further detail of some interest is the presto marking for BWV 1056/3. It occurs much less frequently in Bach's music than is generally thought and significantly, when it does, in the final movements of cyclic chamber ensemble works with solo violin.[79] This offers additional support for assigning the solo melody part in BWV 1056[a]/3 to the violin.

Butler in several concerto movements datable before 1718 ("Towards a More Precise Chronology for Bach's Concerto for Three Violins and Strings," in BOW, 236–45). In these early works, it concerns first movements in $\frac{4}{4}$ measure, compositionally very distant from the strict four-measure periods and dance character of BWV 1056/3. From this perspective, it seems that the "various alternative formal [concerto] structures" with which Bach experimented "from about 1717/18 to at least 1726" (ibid., 245) also included dancelike AB forms, to which a piece such as BWV 1059[a]/3–BWV 35/5 also belongs.

75. On the passepied, see Meredith Little and Natalie Jenne, *Dance and the Music of J. S. Bach* (Bloomington: Indiana University Press, 2001), 83–91.

76. ". . . Unruhe und Wanckelmüthigkeit," Johann Mattheson, *Der vollkommene Capellmeister* (Hamburg, 1739), 229.

77. They are to be found in the fifth English Suite (BWV 810) (c. 1720); the Ouverture in C Major (BWV 1066) (c. 1720); the F-Major Fugue (BWV 856/2) from *Well-Tempered Clavier* I (1722); Inventio 3 (BWV 774) (1723); the Sonata for Violin and Cembalo in F Minor (BWV 1018) (by 1725); the Concerto for Violin, Strings, and Continuo in E Major (BWV 1042) (c. 1725? [see note 77]); the fifth Partita (BWV 829) (1730); the French Ouverture (BWV 831a) (c. 1730); and the E-Major and B-Minor Fugues (BWV 878/2 and 893/2) from the *Well-Tempered Clavier* II (c. 1739).

78. On this new date, see (from two entirely different perspectives) Butler, "J. S. Bach's Reception of the Mature Concertos of Tomaso Albinoni," 42n36, and Payne, "Telemann's Musical Style, c. 1709–c. 1730 and J. S. Bach," 51–57.

79. These are the fourth movement of the Sonata for Solo Violin in G Minor (BWV 1001), the fourth movement of the Partita for Solo Violin in B Minor (BWV 1002), the fourth movement of the Sonata for Violin and Cembalo in A Major (BWV 1015), the fourth movement of the Sonata for Violin and

The G-Minor Violin Concerto is probably Bach's most condensed instrumental concerto. Its short movements, together with the economic use of its thematic material, link it to a certain tendency notable in the instrumental music of the late Köthen period toward compact forms. The most striking works in this respect are the preludes and fugues of the *Well-Tempered Clavier* I of 1722, which are far removed from the much longer preludes, fugues, and toccatas for keyboard of the Weimar period. The phenomenon also appears in Bach's suites; the long English Suites, which probably originated in the late Weimar and early Köthen years, give way to the much smaller-scale French Suites now thought to originate during the years 1721–25. Those concertos likely to have been written in Weimar—BWV 1050a, BWV 1051, BWV 1052a, and BWV 1064[a]—belong without exception to the most extended essays by Bach in this genre, whereas those written in Leipzig, BWV 971 and BWV 1043, belong to the most condensed. From this perspective, the G-Minor Concerto from the Köthen years stands closer to the Leipzig than to the Weimar period. In two important compositional projects from the year 1723, the idea of formal compression reaches a peak—the concentrated *Inventions and Sinfonias*, of which the fair copy was completed in Köthen[80] in early 1723, and the unusually short choruses and arias of the *Magnificat* (BWV 243a), written in June/July of the same year in Leipzig.[81]

There is concrete evidence to support the dating of the G-Minor Concerto to the end of the Köthen period along with the *Inventions and Sinfonias*. The head of the theme of the third movement is closely related to the opening of the chorus "Aller Augen warten, Herr" from the cantata *Du wahrer Gott und Davids Sohn* (BWV 23). (See Examples 9a and 9b.)

BWV 23 was definitely one of Bach's last Köthen compositions, one of two test pieces performed on February 7, 1723, as part of Bach's audition for the post of Leipzig Thomascantor. The major part of this cantata, including the chorus in question, was in all probability composed during the preceding month in Köthen.[82] Originally conceived as the final movement of a three-part, concerto-like cantata,[83] the move-

---

Continuo in G Major (BWV 1021), the third movement of the Sonata for Flute and Cembalo in B Minor (BWV 1030), and the third movement of the Fourth Brandenburg Concerto (BWV 1049).

80. The autograph (P 610) is dated 1723, and Bach's signature carries the title "Hochf. Anhalt.-Cöthnischen Capellmeister." He officially became Leipzig Thomascantor in April of that year.

81. On this new dating relating BWV 243a firmly to the feast of the Visitation of Mary on July 2, 1723, see Andreas Glöckner, "Bachs Es-Dur-Magnificat BWV 243a—ein genuine Weihnachtsmusik?" BJ 89 (2003): 37–45.

82. See Wolff, "Bach's Audition for the St. Thomas Cantorate," 128–35.

83. Ibid., 131.

Ex. 9a. BWV 23/3, *thema*

Ex. 9b. BWV 1056/3, *thema*

ment in question is written in a "standard" concerto form. The "refrain" of the chorus represents the ritornello, which, as is typical of a ritornello-form concerto movement, passes through several keys, while the "couplets" are sung by two soloists. Moreover, as the opening aria, "Du wahrer Gott und Davids Sohn," is dominated by sixteenth-note triplets, an overall conceptual relationship with BWV 1056[a] seems likely. Although it would be naive to base a dating of BWV 1056[a]/3 purely on its thematic resemblance to BWV 23/3, in conjunction with the observations made here, it is tempting to situate the origins of the G-Minor Concerto in close chronological proximity to BWV 23, that is, at the beginning of 1723.

It is likely that BWV 1056[a] formed the final stage in an important phase of Bach's development as a composer of concertos, just before his compositional activity during the first Leipzig years was to be dominated almost exclusively by the composition of church cantatas. The G-Minor Concerto is exemplary in this regard, forming as it does an outstanding example of the compositional mastery and flexibility Bach had achieved in this genre by the end of the Köthen period. Just as do the *Inventions and Sinfonias* to Bach's Köthen keyboard music, so does BWV 1056[a], with its extreme concision, represent a fitting culmination to Bach's Köthen concerted chamber music.

The *Sonate auf Concertenart*

A Postmodern Invention?

David Schulenberg

I t has long been evident that certain sonatas (as well as preludes and other in-strumental compositions) of J. S. Bach and certain of his contemporaries bear resemblances to works with the title *Concerto*. From this it has been inferred that at least some of these pieces were written in imitation of actual concertos. The case was bolstered by the discovery that the eighteenth-century theorist Johann Adolph Scheibe (1708–76) seems to have identified precisely this sort of sonata as a special type, thereby confirming modern perceptions of both genres. Accordingly, a number of scholars have interpreted various works of Bach and his contemporaries not only as concerto parallels, but as more or less conscious efforts to blend genres or generic references.

Without denying the possibility of mixed genres as a device of modern analysis, this essay examines the historical status and significance of the concerto as a genre for German musicians, especially Bach, during the first two decades of the eighteenth century. This may seem a peculiar aim, given the large number of works composed during this period under the title *Concerto* and the firm place of the concerto in our understanding of eighteenth-century music history. But a reexamination of the issue, prompted by recent investigations of Scheibe's *Sonate auf Concertenart*, suggests new ways of understanding how and why composers such as Bach and Telemann incorpo-rated elements now associated with the concerto into their own early works. It also leads to alternate ways of interpreting movements whose designs are now usually understood as ritornello forms, a type identified almost axiomatically with the con-certo in modern writings. I will argue that during the first decades of the eighteenth century, Bach and many of his contemporaries indeed created instrumental works of

This is a revised and expanded version of a paper first presented at the April 1998 meeting of the American Bach Society and then again in November of the same year at the national convention of the American Musicological Society. My research was supported by a William Scheide research grant from the American Bach Society, for which I am most grateful. I also thank Peter Williams and the members of the Harvard Bach Colloquium for reading and commenting on early versions of this paper.

diverse formal and generic patterns. But only gradually did the formal procedures of some of the more prolific writers of such music (Bach being distinctly *not* among them) harden into the relatively rigid patterns that were codified by theorists of the next generation and subsequently enshrined in current views of late-Baroque musical genres.

The first question, therefore, and the one posed in my title, is whether the *Sonate auf Concertenart* was in fact recognized as a distinct genre during Bach's life, particularly at the time when he is thought to have composed several works that have been identified as examples of this genre.[1] As the term *Sonate auf Concertenart* has come into scholarly currency, a growing body of diverse works has been claimed as representative of the type. But has Scheibe's expression been elevated from a term of limited application to a broad category—in effect, an invented genre where none existed in Bach's day? A number of scholars have demonstrated beyond any question that many early eighteenth-century German instrumental works occupy what is understood today as a gray area between the sonata and the concerto. In some cases, different sources assign the same work to different categories; some composers, notably Telemann, wrote chamber works whose title, form, and style seem to reflect a conscious modeling on what is now viewed as the orchestral genre of the concerto.[2]

1. The term *Sonate auf Concertenart* seems to have been first used by Scheibe in the seventy-fourth installment of his *Critischer Musikus*, first published 20 January 1740 and reissued in revised form as part of the work's *neue, vermehrte und verbesserte Auflage* (Leipzig: Bernhard Christoph Breitkopf, 1745; facs. Hildesheim: Olms, 1970), 675–83. Relevant extracts from Scheibe's work are given in the appendix; see extracts 4–7 for his introduction of the term *Sonate auf Concertenart* and most substantial discussion thereof. The first to apply Scheibe's term to specific works of J. S. Bach was apparently Hans Eppstein, *Studien über J. S. Bach's Sonaten für ein Melodieinstrument und obligates Cembalo* (Uppsala: Almqvist & Wiksells, 1966), 46. But Scheibe's concept was first explored in depth by Michael Marissen, "A Trio in C Major for Recorder, Violin, and Continuo by J. S. Bach?" *Early Music* 13 (1985): 384–90. Later studies cited here include Marissen, "A Critical Reappraisal of J. S. Bach's A-Major Flute Sonata," *Journal of Musicology* 6 (1988): 367–86; Laurence Dreyfus, "J. S. Bach and the Status of Genre: Problems of Style in the G-Minor Sonata BWV 1029," *Journal of Musicology* 5 (1987): 57–64, subsequently incorporated into his *Bach and the Patterns of Invention* (Cambridge, Mass.: Harvard University Press, 1996), 103ff.; Jeanne Swack, "On the Origins of the *Sonate auf Concertenart*," *Journal of the American Musicological Society* 46 (1993): 369–414, and Jeanne Swack, "J. S. Bach's A-Major Flute Sonata BWV 1032 Revisited," in *Bach Studies* 2, ed. Daniel R. Melamed (Cambridge: Cambridge University Press, 1995), 154–74; and Steven David Zohn, "The Ensemble Sonatas of Georg Philipp Telemann: Studies in Style, Genre, and Chronology" (Ph.D. diss., Cornell Univ., 1995), 428–531. I am grateful to Steven Zohn for furnishing a prepublication copy "The *Sonate auf Concertenart* and Conceptions of Genre in the Late Baroque," *Journal of Eighteenth-Century Music* 1 (2004): 205–47, which is in part a response to drafts and aural presentations of the present essay.

2. See especially Swack, "On the Origins," 382–87.

Examples 1 and 2 illustrate two such works.[3] Both incorporate features often mentioned as characteristic of the *Sonate auf Concertenart*; in particular, the first movement of each is primarily in a homophonic texture in which, at least initially, one of the upper instrumental lines is set apart as a quasi-soloist while the remaining parts function analogously to an orchestral tutti. But whereas in this view the term *Sonate auf Concertenart* implies the use of formal procedures now associated with the eighteenth-century solo concerto, the criteria actually stated by Scheibe point to more local or superficial features—the absence of an opening slow movement, the omission of imitative counterpoint, and the domination of the texture by one part.[4] In fact, Laurence Dreyfus has criticized the reflexive application of the "metaphor of 'genre as form,'"[5] leading one to ask how useful it is to understand the works in question as alluding to idealized musical genres chiefly through what we perceive as their formal procedures.

The evidence admits a different interpretation. The sonata and the concerto were not clearly distinct genres during the first decade or two of the eighteenth century when Bach, Telemann, and their contemporaries were beginning to compose their works for instrumental ensemble. Rather, the two terms, if not exactly synonymous, at first bore only slightly differing connotations, emerging as labels for truly distinct genres during the course of these composers' careers, after each had already written a substantial portion of his output under both titles *Sonata* and *Concerto*. Hence, far from having been intended to blend or allude to disparate genres, it may be that the works in question simply happened to employ varieties of form, scoring, and other musical elements that would later become identified with the genres with which we now associate them.

As is well known, both sonatas and concertos had existed from the beginning of the seventeenth century, but only during the last decades of the century does the term *concerto* seem to have been first applied to purely instrumental works. Torelli published his op. 6 *Concerti* (Augsburg, 1698) while he was at Ansbach, where his pupils included the young Pisendel—so by 1700, *Concerto* was certainly familiar to some Germans

---

3. Swack, ibid., 405, notes the close similarities between the two works, observing, incidentally, that it is impossible to say which one might have preceded or influenced the other. One copy of Graun's trio in A (Example 1), no. 8 in the thematic catalog by Matthias Wendt, is dated about 1740, suggesting that this work was composed later than Bach's; see Matthias Wendt, "Die Trios der Brüder Johann Gottlieb und Carl Heinrich Graun" (Ph.D. diss., Rheinische Friedrich-Wilhelms-Universität, Bonn, 1983), 257–58.

4. Thus Ute Poetzsch, preface to *Georg Philipp Telemann: Konzerte und Sonaten für 2 Violinen, Viola und Basso Continuo. Georg Philipp Telemann: Musikalische Werke* 28 (Kassel: Bärenreiter, 1995), viii.

5. See his discussion of fugue (*Bach and the Patterns of Invention*, 135).

as a title for an instrumental composition. But these and other early concertos show few of the features that we associate with the term, and German musicians and their audiences may not have understood the instrumental concerto as a distinct genre of music until the second decade of the eighteenth century. Indeed, even in the 1720s and later, the terms *sonata* and *concerto* were still sometimes applied in ways that are now hard to understand, although the title *Concerto* was becoming limited to works that employed what copyists and writers of the period called *concertato* parts.[6] To borrow a phrase from Alexander Silbiger, the sonata and concerto for a while may have formed a genre pair, like the chaconne and passacaglia. But whereas the evolution of the latter pair converged, the sonata and concerto were in the process of diverging during the first few decades of the eighteenth century.[7]

This is not to say that before 1720 or so the two genres were never distinguished from each other. Torelli had alternated concertos with sonatas in his opus 5 (1692), a practice imitated by Albinoni in his *Sinfonie a cinque* op. 2 (which consists of six concertos and six sonatas) of 1700. Bach knew at least one item from the latter set; his copy of the basso continuo part for op. 2 no. 2 survives in Leipzig. The concertos of this set include an additional ripieno violin part whose presence permits new variations of texture, including solo passages for the principal violin. But the latter are not the basis for the formal design of any movements. By 1720, there did exist a substantial repertory of what we now call solo concertos, that is, instrumental works in several movements in which one or more *concertato* parts are clearly set against a larger group of ripieno parts. But other types of work continued to be known by the same title, including the varieties now distinguished as *concerti grossi* and *concerti ripieni*—the first comprising, essentially, trio sonatas expanded by the addition of ripieno instruments in selected passages (on the Roman model established by Corelli), the latter comprising works for string ensemble without separate *concertato* parts. Nowadays it is assumed that the *concertato* parts play distinct solo episodes characterized by virtuoso passage-work in the quick movements of a concerto, and that they receive opportunities for expressive embellishment (whether improvised or written out) in the slow movements. One expects, too, that at least the quick movements will be structured according to ritornello form. But none of these suppositions enters into the earliest discussions of

6. Although in current usage the term *concertato* (and its English equivalent *concerted*) is often applied to genres, one rarely discovers such a thing as a "concerted fugue" in eighteenth-century titles; rather, one finds concerted violin or harpsichord *parts*, that is, obbligato or solo parts. It is, then, anachronistic to use the adjective *concerted* to mean "in the style of a concerto."

7. See Alexander Silbiger, "Passacaglia and Ciaccona: Genre Pairing and Ambiguity from Frescobaldi to Couperin," *Journal of Seventeenth-Century Music* 2, no. 1 (Dec. 1996) <http://sscm-jscm.press.uiuc.edu/jscm/v2/no1/silbiger.html>, para. 5.2.

the instrumental concerto as a genre. The concerto and the sonata would have had to be established as clearly distinct genres before composers could have alluded to one or the other for genre-crossing purposes. However, it is unclear that the chronology of the development of instrumental music in the early eighteenth century would have allowed for this.

My proposal, if true, would have some bearing on our interpretations of both the music and the theoretical writings of the period. Rather than understanding a work such as Bach's Sonata for Viola da Gamba and Cembalo in G Minor (BWV 1029), as incorporating "a synthesis of concerto and sonata principles,"[8] we might see it as employing a fluid combination of compositional techniques and musical signs that only later crystallized to represent separate and distinct formal principles. Rather than seeing conscious, explicit, references to the concerto in certain sonatas, we would instead see composers such as Bach using, not only in concertos but in sonatas, preludes, and other genres, a variety of compositional devices that only later became particularly associated with one genre or another. Among these devices are ritornello form and the *Devisen* entrance, which have become closely associated with the concerto in music historiography despite their origins in the aria.[9]

My proposal is not intended to rule out the presence of sophisticated intergeneric references in Bach's chamber works and other late Baroque music. But although interpretations along such lines may be unimpeachable as modern hearings of this repertory, they do not necessarily reflect the composer's intentions or the ways in which a contemporary listener would have understood the works in question. To be sure, we lack clear windows into early eighteenth-century ways of hearing these pieces, but theoretical and critical writings, as well as titles and part rosters in original sources, provide a glimpse. From these it is evident that even the division between solo and tutti, so fundamental to modern views of the concerto, was relatively insignificant from some early eighteenth-century perspectives. Hence apparent *allusions* to the solo–tutti distinction may not have served as markers of the concerto in works such as the two sonatas illustrated in Examples 1 and 2. Indeed, which if any of what are now thought to be the conventions of concerto writing were well defined around 1713, when Bach is thought to have begun transcribing instrumental concertos for keyboard instruments?[10]

---

8. Dreyfus, *Bach and the Patterns of Invention,* 106.

9. Arguably, some composers of instrumental music adopted such vocal devices indirectly, from other instrumental music. For example, Gregory G. Butler, "J. S. Bach's Reception of Tomaso Albinoni's Mature Concertos," in *Bach Studies* 2, ed. Daniel R. Melamed (Cambridge: Cambridge University Press, 1995), 24–25, traces the use of a "double *Devise*" in Bach's concerto movements not to "his own da capo aria" but to the "characteristic" use of this technique in the later concertos of Albinoni.

10. The now customary dating of these works depends on the argument of Hans-Joachim Schulze

The problem deepens when one attempts to identify precisely which passages in a given sonata movement correspond to the tutti and solo passages—that is, the ritornellos and the solo episodes—of an archetypal concerto movement. The exercise often begins simply, as in the outset of the two works shown in Examples 1 and 2. But as the music proceeds, different listeners are apt to reach different conclusions as to which passage represents which part of a concerto.[11] The problem is not confined to works of J. S. Bach, and although it might be ascribed to deliberate genre blurring, it is logical at least to reconsider the underlying premise that individual passages in such movements serve as functional equivalents for either the "solo" or the "tutti" (or "ritornello") sections of a concerto.

Genres in Theory

The view that certain sonatas by Bach and others refer to the concerto genre rests on the assumption that instrumental concertos have (or had) some generally agreed-upon set of characteristics that can (or could) be readily presented by a composer and perceived by a listener. The tutti–solo alternation seems one such characteristic; another is the set of procedures that we conveniently call ritornello form. Yet early eighteenth-century sources provide only weak support for such views, and then only by implication. Walther and Mattheson speak of ritornellos only within the context of the aria, and for Scheibe the now-familiar application of the word *ritornello* to concerto movements remains an extension of its proper meaning.[12] Only in another discussion does Scheibe refer to those passages "most characteristic of the concerto"—by which he probably means soloistic passagework, not ritornellos.

As Peter Williams has observed, "Ritornello forms in J. S. Bach's sonatas, preludes, and fugues follow their own line of development, seldom clearly based on, derived from, or even paralleled by particular movements of Vivaldi."[13] Whether such move-

---

that Bach's opportunities for studying and playing the works of Vivaldi and others probably broadened considerably in 1713, when Prince Johann Ernst of Sachsen-Weimar returned from university studies in Utrecht; see his *Studien zur Bach-Überlieferung im 18. Jahrhundert* (Leipzig: Edition Peters, 1984), 146ff. Karl Heller raises the possibility of Bach's work having taken place over a more extended period, noting the existence of alternate versions; see Karl Heller, ed., NBA V,11 (*Bearbeitungen fremder Werke: Concerti* BWV 972–87, 592a; *Sonaten* BWV 965, 966, *Fuga* BWV 954), KB, 18–19. One might also point to considerable differences in the degree to which the individual concertos are reworked for keyboard performance.

11. See, for example, the differing analyses of the first movement of BWV 1032 by Marissen and Swack in the articles cited in note 1.

12. The main or opening passage of a concerto is only *gleichsam*, "as it were," a ritornello (see appendix in this chapter, extract 2).

13. Peter Williams, *The Organ Music of J. S. Bach*, 2nd ed. (Cambridge: Cambridge University Press, 2003), 204.

Ex. 1. J. G. Graun, *Trio per il Flauto Trav: Violino e Basso* in A (Wendt 8), first mvt. (opening).

Ex. 1. Continued.

Ex. 2. J. S. Bach, Sonata for Flute and Cembalo in A Major (BWV 1032),
first mvt. (opening).

ments were regarded as specifically concerto-like may be doubted, however, for many early eighteenth-century works titled *concerto* do not consistently employ ritornello form or tutti–solo alternation. It is by no means uncommon to find early concertos in which only the first quick movement has anything like a ritornello structure, and even then its design may be far from that given in modern textbooks on the basis of certain movements from Vivaldi concertos. No doubt the form of the first quick movement is particularly important in defining the genre of the work as a whole, if only because this is usually the longest, most complex movement. Nevertheless, one must question whether formal design was involved in the genre categories of early eighteenth-century theorists and—insofar as we can judge it—of composers and listeners.

More fundamentally, however, it is by no means clear how the early instrumental concerto was understood to differ from the contemporary sonata. Hence, from a historical point of view, the crucial question is when the two did diverge. When Bach was composing the works now known as the Brandenburg Concertos, did he think of them as concertos? If so, did that expression imply a distinct contrast to other works designated as sonatas? Were there, for example, formal elements characteristic of one genre but not the other? If one heard something resembling a ritornello in a sonata, would one have heard this as a reference to a foreign genre, or would this simply have been an ordinary formal procedure, one ultimately derived from the aria, perhaps, but not yet associated with concertos and employed in sonatas as a special effect?

The Generic Status of Scheibe's *Sonate auf Concertenart*

If the *Sonate auf Concertenart* had been a widely recognized genre, one would expect it to have been documented in various historical sources. But although modern commentators have found many compositions that seem to belong to such a category, Scheibe is the only writer to have used the term. His description, in a single chapter of a large theoretical work, is far from clear on many points and cites not a single specific composition. Even if he accurately reflects the perceptions of an intelligent listener of the late 1730s, the relevant works of Bach were composed at times and in circumstances that remain uncertain and, in any case, they cannot be precisely fitted to Scheibe's description.[14]

Scheibe's failure to name specific pieces is in keeping with his and other eighteenth-century music theorists' tendency to write normatively. Although ostensibly a figure of the *Aufklärung*, Scheibe tends toward a prescriptive nominalism that leads him habitually to essentialize categories that are based more on theoretical invention than empirical description. Thus he distinguishes genres (*Gattungen*) by stating how each "must" go.[15] Jeanne Swack points out that Scheibe "does not treat the *Sonate auf*

14. As noted by Dreyfus, *Bach and the Patterns of Invention*, 106.

15. One might note the frequent use of the verb *müssen* in the quotations found in the appendix in

Concertenart as an obscure or even uncommon genre,"[16] but it does not follow that Scheibe's term had wide currency. Although eighteenth-century theorists were wont to define numerous categories and subcategories of music, the more idiosyncratic terms did not necessarily find general usage.[17]

There must also be some question as to how specifically the last two words of Scheibe's phrase refer to the concerto as a genre, for the expression had an older usage relating to the venerable distinction between concertists and ripienists.[18] In that case, *auf Concertenart* might mean little more than "in the manner of a solo." But it is hard to believe that by the 1730s readers would not have thought of actual concertos in this connection, and even if they had, what would have seemed to them to be the defining features of such works? Scheibe was apparently the first theorist to describe the ritornello as an element in quick concerto movements. For Scheibe, a concerto opens with a *Hauptsatz* in which the *Concertstimme* may or may not play, as the composer determines ("Das ist nun gleichsam das Rittornel"); the latter alternates with *Zwischensätze*.[19] It is clear that Scheibe understands such a concerto movement by analogy to the aria, and it is in keeping with his schematic, normalizing approach that his descriptions of the two forms contain striking parallelisms.[20] But although the

---

this chapter. For example, Scheibe's account of the solo sonata includes at one point six sentences in a row that each prescribe something about how such a work "must" proceed (681–82). This is in keeping with the project of rationalist aesthetics, announced at the outset of the *Versuch einer Critische Dichtkunst* of Johann Christoph Gottsched, to "evaluate and examine objects according to fundamental rules that are germane to the thing under consideration" (ii). Gottsched's work was consulted in the *4. vermehrten Auflage* (Leipzig: Breitkopf, 1751; facs. Darmstadt: Wissenschaftliche Buchgesellschaft, 1962).

16. "On the Origins," 372–73.

17. Walther's *Lexicon*, for example, gives terms for varieties of fugue found almost nowhere else; see Stefan Kunze, "Gattungen der Fuge in Bachs Wohltemperierten Klavier," in *Bach-Interpretation*, ed. Martin Geck (Göttingen: Vandenhoeck und Ruprecht, 1969), 74–93.

18. In the preface to his *Musica boscareccia* (Strassburg, 1632), a collection of songs for three voices and continuo, Johann Hermann Schein referred to the possibility of omitting the two lower voices and performing the works *"auff Concertenart,"* that is, as monodies. (This is misunderstood by R. Hinton Thomas, *Poetry and Song in the German Baroque: A Study of the Continuo Lied* [Oxford: Clarendon Press, 1963], 30, when Thomas supposes that Schein is referring to "the question of choral performance.") Although a direct relationship between Schein and Scheibe is unlikely, the underlying principle is consistent with Walther and Mattheson's sense of *concerto* as relating to soloistic or monodic texture.

19. 631–32; see appendix in this chapter, extract 2.

20. On the aria: "Ueberhaupt aber kann man in dieser Art von Arien die Geigen so vielfach bestellen, als man will, und als man denket, daß es der Stärke, oder der Schwäche, der Singestimme gemäß

parallels between the two genres may seem obvious to us, they find no recognition in the encyclopedic works of Scheibe's immediate predecessors Mattheson and Walther.[21] And only in much later accounts—those of Riepel and, especially, Koch—does the modern view emerge of concerto movements as formal and, to some degree, expressive or dramatic counterparts of the ritornello-form aria.[22]

We might attribute the cursory nature of the earlier accounts to the conservatism typical of lexicographic writings in general. In 1713, Mattheson, for example, still viewed the strophic aria as the norm and the ritornello of an aria as falling properly between its stanzas despite the predominance of da capo form in contemporary arias, including his own.[23] But even Scheibe, in his discussion of the *Sonate auf Concertenart*, refers not to form but to texture as the basic criterion of the genre: what matters above all is that one instrument stands apart and above the rest, dominating the ensemble.[24] This is an echo of Walther and Mattheson's understanding of the concerto.[25] That

---

ist" (431–32); and on the concerto: "Wenn in der Arie der Affect und die Worte dem Componisten an gewisse Anmerkungen binden: so hat er hingegen im Concerte auf die Stärke des Instruments und auf die Ausführung seines zum Grunde gelegten Hauptsatzes zu sehen" (632). Likewise, "Was also daselbst von der Singstimme bemerket worden, das kann, mit veränderten Unständen, auf die Concertstimme ausgeleget werden" (ibid.).

21. The definitions of *ritornello* given by Walther and Mattheson refer only to vocal music; see Walther, *Praecepta der musicalischen Composition* (lost ms. dated 1708), ed. Peter Benary (Leipzig: VEB Breitkopf und Härtel, 1955); Walther, *Musicalisches Lexicon oder musikalische Bibliothec* (Leipzig: Wolffgang Deer, 1732; facs. ed. Richard Schaal, Kassel: Bärenreiter, 1953); and Mattheson, *Das neu-eröffnete Orchestre* (Hamburg: Benjamin Schillers Wittwe, 1713).

22. Joseph Riepel, *Anfangsgründe zur musikalischen Setzkunst*, 5 vols. (Regensburg, 1752–68), esp. 2:93ff (1:199ff in facsimile in *Joseph Riepel: Sämtliche Schriften zur Musiktheorie*, ed. Thomas Emmerig [Vienna: Böhlau, 1996], 2 vols.); and Heinrich Christoph Koch, *Versuch einer Anleitung zur Composition*, 3 vols. (Leipzig, 1782–93), ii.4.4.1.10.120 (210 in the partial translation by Nancy Kovaleff Baker as *Introductory Essay on Composition: The Mechanical Rules of Melody, Sections 3 and 4* [New Haven, Conn.: Yale University Press, 1983]). On Koch, see Jane Stevens, "An Eighteenth-Century Description of Concerto First-Movement Form," *Journal of the American Musicological Society* 24 (1971): 85–95.

23. Mattheson, *Das neu-eröffnete Orchestre*, 183–84. Strophic arias remain common in German cantatas from the first two decades of the eighteenth century, as in the works by Telemann and Heinichen cited below.

24. "Ein Concert aber ist ein solches Stück, in welchem ein Instrument oder mehrere Instrumente, unter den übrigen Instrumenten, die ihnen zur Begleitung zugegeben werden, auf eine außerordentliche Art hervorragen, also, daß sie zugleich ihre Eigenschaft durch besondere Sätze bezeigen, und dadurch den andern sie begleitenden Instrumenten gleichsam den Vorzug abstreiten" (630–31).

25. The definition of *concerto* in Walther's *Lexicon* is openly derived from that of Mattheson's *Orchestre*, which Walther cites. The crucial phrase in Mattheson reads: "auch in solchen Sachen und anderen / wo nur die erste *Partie* dominiret / und wo unter vielen *Violinen*, eine mit sonderlicher Hurtigkeit

65

texture rather than form was crucial for both Mattheson and Walther is evident from the latter's understanding of the word *concertato*, the expression applied by both authors to the dominating part.[26] Evidently, for all three writers, form in the modern sense held little theoretical interest. Scheibe's account of the *Sonate auf Concertenart* refers to it only obliquely in its prescription of "variegated" and "convoluted" melodic lines for what we might call the soloistic sections of a movement in concerto style.

These terms, translated from the German *verändernd* and *kräuselnd*, are unfortunately just two among many vague expressions that make Scheibe's writings difficult to apply to actual music.[27] Scheibe twice indicates that sonatas *auf Concertenart* can employ *kräuselnde* and *verändernde Sätze*, without making himself any clearer than that. He repeatedly prescribes melodies that are *fließend* and *bündig* for "ordinary" sonatas (bass parts are also to be *bündig*), without specifying how this is achieved. Elsewhere Scheibe speaks of "those places which above others inherently constitute the essence of the concerto." Modern writers have assumed that this refers to ritornellos, but in fact Scheibe must be referring to solo episodes.[28] His terms *eigentlich* ("inherently" or "intrinsically") and *Wesen* ("essence") refer, in a pedantically Aristotelian manner, to that which defines the concerto—that is, what distinguishes it from other types of music. For Scheibe, it is the presence of soloists (*concertato* parts) that does this, just as in "ordinary" sonatas it is the fugal working-out of a "regular melody."[29] Thus it must be what we call solo episodes and not ritornellos that define (are "essential" to)

---

hervorrafet / dieselbe / *Violino concertino*, genennet wird." Previously, in his 1708 *Praecepta*, Walther's definition had given only the sense of a competitive instrumental piece, drawing on the familiar pseudo-etymology: "*Concerto (ital.:)* ein künstlich gesetztes Stück, worinnen die Stimmen gleichsam mit einander in die Wette streiten. *lat: Concertatio*" (110; 43 in mod. ed.).

26. Walther's 1732 definition of the term *concertante* begins with a direct translation of that given for *concertato* by the French lexicographer Sébastien de Brossard (*Dictionaire de musique*, 3rd ed. [Amsterdam, ca. 1710]): "Ce mot se met avec le nom de toutes les Parties *Recitantes* pour les distinguer des Parties qui ne chantent que dans le gros Chœur." To this Walther adds: "Es geschiehet auch solches in Instrumental Sachen." Matthias Wendt discusses usage of the term *concertato* in "Solo—Obligato—Concertato: Fakten zur Terminologie der konzertierenden Instrumentalpartien bei Johann Sebastian Bach," in *Beiträge zur Geschichte des Konzerts: Festschrift Siegfried Kross zum 60. Geburtstag*, ed. Reinhard Emans and Matthias Wendt (Bonn: Gudrun Schröder, 1990), 57–76.

27. See appendix, extracts 5 and 7. I use Swack's translation of *kräuselnd*, from "On the Origins," 371.

28. See appendix, extract 3, and compare Scheibe's use of the same phrase several pages earlier (extract 1): "die Hauptstimmen, oder die concertirenden Stimmen spielen, und also das Wesen des Concerts eigentlich ausmachen." The parallelism, fairly obvious when reading the original, may have been overlooked because only the second passage appears, quoted as part of a paragraph relevant to Bach, in NBR, 331–32.

29. See appendix, extract 5.

the concerto.[30] But Scheibe's neat distinction between works *auf Concertenart* and *auf Fugenart* is belied by the pervasive use of permutational structures not only in Bach's concertos, but in concertos with multiple soloists by Vivaldi and others. Indeed, Scheibe recognizes that the distinction breaks down in concertos with multiple soloists.[31]

Thus one must wonder to what degree the presence of distinct solo episodes really did characterize the concerto to the exclusion of other types of instrumental music, particularly during the first decades of the century. This is so even when writers clearly refer—as Mattheson and Scheibe certainly do—to what we call solo concertos, as opposed to the concerto grosso or the so-called "group concerto." The archetypal solo violin sonatas of Corelli include several movements resembling what are now sometimes termed *concertante* fugues, in which one or more episodes are made up of passagework that we tend to view as concerto-like.[32] The fugues in Bach's three sonatas for unaccompanied violin follow similar designs, and numerous commentators have pointed to comparable patterns in many of Bach's organ preludes. Yet it does not follow that the organ preludes were modeled on concerto movements, for, as Williams suggests, the underlying formal principle is more universal than that.

For Scheibe, the essential difference between sonatas and concertos may actually have lain not in their overall designs but in the more contrapuntal texture (and thus more conservative style) of the sonata. Indeed, Scheibe's word *Concertenart* is best understood in opposition to his *Fugenart*, which for him is the appropriate manner for the first quick movement of an "ordinary" sonata (see the appendix accompanying this chapter, extract 7). The sense of the sonata as normally contrapuntal and therefore old-fashioned may also lie behind Mattheson's 1713 view that the sonata "has almost begun to seem outdated, rather supplanted and replaced by the new, so-called concertos and suites."[33] Ironically, within a few years German composers (including

---

30. Marissen, in both "A Trio" and "A Critical Appraisal," supplements Scheibe's expression "those passages" by identifying the latter as the ritornellos (he quotes the translation of Scheibe's passage from NBR, 331–32). He is followed by Dreyfus (*Bach and the Patterns of Invention*, 105), Zohn ("The Ensemble Sonatas," 437), and Swack, who views the ritornello as "the concerto's most distinctive marker" while regarding the exchange of material between parts as "more typical of the conventional trio sonata" ("Bach's A-Major Flute Sonata," 159).

31. ". . . folglich muss man auch dazu die Regeln der Fuge, des doppelten und drey-oder vierfachen Contrapuncts, und auch wohl des Canons anwenden" (635). By "permutational structures" I refer to contrapuntal solo episodes that recur in the course of a movement with their counterpoint inverted, as in the *Stimmtausch* heard repeatedly in the first movement of the Second Brandenburg Concerto.

32. The term was popularized in a frequently cited article by Carl Dahlhaus, "Bachs konzertante Fugen," BJ 41 (1955): 45–72.

33. ". . . nunmehro schier etwas zu veralten beginnen will / und von den neuern so genanten *Concerten* und *Suiten* ziemlich ausgestochen und hinangesetzet" (*Orchestre*, 175).

Mattheson) were publishing numerous sonatas in an up-to-date style that avoided serious counterpoint.

To what degree Mattheson or Scheibe's contemporaries shared their perceptions remains to be elucidated. But the fact that we so strongly associate ritornello form with the so-called Vivaldian concerto does not mean that Bach and other musicians of the time did the same. As Michael Talbot points out in his sketch of the early history of the instrumental concerto in Italy, Mattheson's account of 1713 "betrays by its vagueness and cumbersome language the novelty of the genre," whose essence, at first, lay "in the energetic writing for the dominant part . . ., not in solo–tutti contrast as such."[34] Many quick concerto movements are in binary form, particularly in works composed before 1720, and slow movements take all manner of designs. We privilege the quick first movement in what became the standard three-movement concerto by taking its form as a symbol of the whole. But only with Scheibe does one begin to find clear historical evidence for such a view of the concerto. Even then, it is the aria that serves as model for concerto movements, and it can hardly be coincidental that da capo form, the quintessential aria design of the early eighteenth century, is a frequent alternative in works by Bach and Telemann.[35] By the same token, *Devisen* entries and other devices commonly associated with arias are also heard frequently in concertos and concerto-like pieces.

Sonaten auf Concertenart by Bach?

Scheibe's treatise appeared originally in serialized form during the period 1737–40. It was in many ways explicitly modeled on the *Versuch einer Critische Dichtkunst* of the Leipzig professor Johann Christoph Gottsched, Scheibe's teacher, not least in both authors' fundamentally ahistorical, essentialist approach to genre.[36] Given this ap-

---

34. *Tomaso Albinoni: The Venetian Composer and His World* (Oxford: Clarendon Press, 1990), 100. In "The Ensemble Sonatas," 529, Zohn also makes the important point that what he regards as Telemann's early *Sonaten auf Concertenart* and ripieno concertos are modeled not on chamber concertos by Vivaldi but on earlier solo concertos by Torelli, Albinoni, and others active before 1710.

35. Telemann uses da capo forms not only throughout his vast output of sonatas and concertos, but also in suites, works for solo keyboard, and other settings.

36. Gottsched's systematic survey of literary genres, from ancient through modern types (including cantatas, operas, and other forms of musical theater), occupies the second half of the book's 840 pages of text. For a valuable study of the philosophical views underlying the writings of both Gottsched and Scheibe, together with a frank estimation of Scheibe's relative strength as a critical thinker, see Joachim Birke, *Christian Wolffs Metaphysik und die zeitgenössische Literatur- und Musiktheorie: Gottsched, Scheibe, Mizler* (Berlin: Walter de Gruyter, 1966). That Gottsched's genre theory followed from "Wolff's optimistic belief in universal ahistorical categories" is argued in John David Pizer, *The Historical Perspective in German Genre Theory: Its Development from Gottsched to Hegel* (Stuttgart: Hans-Dieter Heinz Akademischer Verlag, 1985), 19–45.

proach and the date of publication, one would hardly be surprised if Scheibe failed to reflect views of twenty or more years earlier, when at least some of Bach's sonatas and concertos were probably first written.[37] Indeed, if we compare sonatas and concertos by members of Scheibe's generation with those of Bach's, we discover indications that the two genres had grown significantly more differentiated by that date, each tending toward greater consistency with respect to such matters as scoring, sequence of movements, and internal formal design of each movement. Thus, by 1740, C. P. E. Bach was consistently using much the same formal scheme for each movement of a concerto or sonata. Such a consistency cannot be found in the earlier works of his father, Vivaldi, or others of their generation. This suggests a certain hardening of once free formal procedures into structural routines.[38]

It is commonly assumed that J. S. Bach's use of such designs stemmed from his arrangements of Vivaldian concertos. But so-called *concertante* fugues can also be found in many sonatas by Telemann, Zelenka, and others written at about the same time, and comparable designs occur in Bach's own early keyboard fugues (notably BWV 579 and 950, on themes by Corelli and Albinoni, respectively).[39] If one requires specific models for these works, the fugues in the first six sonatas in Corelli's op. 5 are probably closer in style and form than the relatively small number of concerto movements with fugal ritornellos.[40]

Many of Bach's earliest keyboard works—that is, ones thought to date from before his arrival at Weimar in 1708—include sections that adopt some sort of rondeau-like structure, in which a recurring theme more or less comparable to a ritornello alternates with other material. In some cases the recurring theme is quite short, as in the first quick passages of several of the *manualiter* toccatas. In other cases a fugue subject may

37. Scheibe probably would have failed to reflect older views even if he did in fact write the relevant portion of his work in consultation with Telemann, a recurring suggestion (see, e.g., Zohn, "The Ensemble Sonatas," 440) for which, however, there is no evidence.

38. On Emanuel Bach's concertos, see my "C. P. E. Bach through the 1740s: The Growth of a Style," in *C. P. E. Bach Studies*, ed. Stephen L. Clark (Oxford: Clarendon Press, 1988), 217–18. The few instrumental compositions of Scheibe accessible to me seem to bear this out; I have been able to consult (through recordings only) two flute concertos from the Raben collection at Aalholm Hall, Denmark, and the *III sonate per il cembalo obligato e flauto traverso o violino concertato*, op. 1 (Nürnberg: Haffner, ca. 1750).

39. Williams, *The Organ Music*, discusses ritornello or concerto-like forms not only in Bach's concerto transcriptions (BWV 592–96), but also in the sonatas (BWV 525–30) and various praeludia, toccatas, and chorale settings, the common theme being skepticism that any one type of composition furnished models for these works.

40. Current perceptions of the significance of fugal ritornellos may have been influenced by their use in several Bach works, including his organ arrangement (BWV 596) of the one example in a quick movement from Vivaldi's op. 3 (Concerto 11 in D Minor, RV 565).

be so long that it seems to function more like a rondeau theme than as the basis for contrapuntal elaboration.[41] It is difficult to speak of concerto influence in such pieces, however, because the style is not particularly close to that of Italian violin music of the period.[42] More plausible as concerto imitations are the preludes of English Suites II–VI (BWV 807–11), which may have been composed as early as 1713 or so, that is, about the same time that Bach is thought to have been arranging concertos by Vivaldi, Telemann, and others for organ and harpsichord.[43] That would seem to clinch the argument; yet these preludes employ da capo forms rarely encountered in Italian concerto movements, and at any rate, textbook ritornello form is by no means the sole principle governing the forms of individual movements in early concertos by Vivaldi and others.[44] Some such design is present in the first quick movement of each of the Venetian concertos that Bach transcribed for keyboard, but these show considerable variety in modulating schemes and other details, as well as in the degree to which the ritornello actually returns as a unit.[45]

Unfortunately, not a single composing score survives for any of the works most frequently cited as *Sonaten auf Concertenart*—the Sonatas for Flute and Cembalo in B Minor and A Major (BWV 1030 and 1032); the G-Minor Gamba Sonata (BWV 1029);

41. Thus in the early Capriccio in E (BWV 993), whose subject alternates with extended episodes comprised primarily of idiomatic figuration; the same is also true of many of Zelenka's unusually long, complex fugue subjects.

42. See, for example, the *manualiter* toccatas and the sonata BWV 967.

43. Alfred Dürr notes that although the earliest sources of the English Suites date from the 1720s, "wir aus stilistischen Gründen auch eine frühere Entstehung—ab etwa 1713—nicht völlig ausschließen können" ("Probleme zur musikalischen Textkritik dargestellt an den Klaviersuiten BWV 806–819 von J. S. Bach," in Alfred Dürr, *Im Mittelpunkt Bach: Ausgewählte Aufsätze und Vorträge* [Kassel: Bärenreiter, 1988], 243). Gregory Butler argues more strongly for the early date in "The Prelude to the Third English Suite BWV 808: An Allegro Concerto Movement in Ritornello Form," in *Bach Studies from Dublin*, ed. Anne Leahy and Yo Tomita (Dublin: Four Courts Press, 2004), 98–100. A striking parallel between the prelude of the third suite and the opening *Fantasie* from Suite 5 (in the same key) in Johann Mattheson's *Pièces de clavecin* also suggests a relatively early date. Mattheson's work appeared in 1714, and its publication in London, with an English title page, might even be the long-disputed reason for the title "English" suites applied to Bach's works. I am grateful to Peter Williams for pointing me toward Mattheson's pieces in connection with J. S. Bach.

44. By "textbook" ritornello form I mean a regular alternation of ritornello and solo episode, these being clearly articulated from one other by scoring, material, and/or texture. The earliest reference to such a form in instrumental music appears to be that of Scheibe, more detailed accounts being given by Johann Joachim Quantz, *Versuch einer Anweisung das Flöte traversiere zu spielen* (Berlin, 1752), and Joseph Riepel, *Anfangsgründe zur musikalischen Setzkunst*.

45. For example, in Vivaldi's op. 3 no. 9 (model for BWV 972), neither quick movement ever restates its opening ritornello.

and the G-Major Organ Sonata (BWV 530). These survive only in fair-copy autographs (*Reinschriften*) or late copies. Equally relevant here are the concertos themselves, which survive only in *Reinschriften* or revision copies, sets of parts, and copies. As a result, we do not know the original titles, dates of composition, or instrumental settings for any of these works. It seems certain, however, that Bach had written a substantial portion of his surviving output of concertos by the early 1720s—in other words, before the hardening of genre definitions alluded to here. It is likely that by 1721, the date of the fair-copy dedication score of the Brandenburg Concertos, Bach had also written other concertos. Direct evidence for this view is scant, but it is supported by arguments based on style and internal evidence[46] and by concerto-like opening movements of a number of cantatas dating from as early as 1713.

Sonaten auf Concertenart in Modern Views

The view of certain compositions as *Sonaten auf Concertenart* depends on criteria derived in part from Scheibe but also through modern analysis. Chief of these is the modern understanding of ritornello form, often characterized as "Vivaldian" because certain concertos by the Venetian composer represent archetypes for the modern view of the form. But other criteria have been advanced, as well, including "orchestral" as opposed to "chamber" scoring, and the use of what Steven Zohn describes as "gestures associated with the concerto."[47] Among the latter are homophonic or unison textures, a "filler" viola part, instrumental recitative, "aria-like slow movements," and a type of binary-form final movement characterized by athletic passagework, often with imitation or voice exchange between the upper parts. Each of these deserves consideration, although earlier musicians did not necessarily share modern perceptions of the markers that characterized instrumental concertos or concerto style.

The most important of these has certainly been ritornello form. What, in fact, is meant by *ritornello form* ("Vivaldian" or otherwise) in modern writings? Minimally, it appears to be almost any material heard at the outset of a piece and repeated later, such as the brief opening phrase played by the tutti at the outset of Vivaldi's Concerto for

46. That at least one of Bach's violin concertos had been composed and was in circulation by 1726 is evident from a list of pieces acquired by the Ulm Collegium Musicum during the 1725–26 season; see Adelheid Krause-Pichler, *Jakob Friedrich Kleinknecht 1722–1794: Ein Komponist zwischen Barock und Klassik* (Weißenhorn: Konrad, 1991), 223–24. That the "Bach" who wrote the "Conc. a viol: Pr: 3. V.V.A. violo. obl. et B" was Johann Sebastian is implied by the presence of a "Concerto Großo" by "Bach" of "Lipsia" in the next season's list.

47. Zohn, "The Ensemble Sonatas," 491–92. At issue is whether ritornello form, "stereotypical orchestral gestures," and other markers indeed constitute "generic reference to the concerto allegro," as Zohn suggests in "The *Sonate auf Concertenart* and Conceptions of Genre."

Flute, Oboe, Violin, Bassoon, and Continuo in G Minor (RV 107).[48] Russell Stinson even speaks of the one-measure fugal subject of the organ chorale *Herr Jesu Christ, dich zu uns wend* (BWV 655) as "a ritornello," and Jean-Claude Zehnder has described equally short passages as *Kurz-Ritornellen* in instrumental works by Torelli and others that Bach might have encountered during the first decade of the eighteenth century.[49]

The word *ritornello* (or its cognates) appears frequently in performing materials from the first two decades of the century, but often attached to instrumental refrains in vocal movements whose style and form recall the old strophic aria.[50] These ritornellos rarely modulate and rarely appear in any key other than the tonic, thus not yet serving one of the essential functions of the "Vivaldian" ritornello, that of confirming new modulations and articulating the large tonal and dramatic structure of a movement. These functions are not absent in German instrumental music of the first two decades of the eighteenth century, but often they are served by fugue subjects or other types of thematic statement shorter than the ritornellos of most Italian arias and are quite different in style. Some movements open with what seems to us a normal ritornello–solo sequence, but these turn out to be rounded binary forms, or they fail to restate the ritornello in other keys, if at all. In other cases—including the works with so-called *Kurz-Ritornellen*—a recurring thematic idea functions as we would expect a ritornello in a later work, but it is so brief that its subsequent statements seem more like temporary interruptions or punctuations of the music than like restatements of a formally crucial ritornello. This occurs not only in works by the first generation of Venetian concerto composers, but in German compositions such as a concerto in D

48. Cited by Swack, "On the Origins," 375. Very brief ritornellos can be found in early eighteenth-century arias, e.g., the three-measure ritornello of the soprano aria "Ich traue Gott" in Telemann's *Gelobet sey der Herr* TWV 1:596 of 1719 (examined in the copy from the Grimma collection in Dl Mus. ms. 2392-E-591). But these are somewhat unusual, and passages actually labeled as ritornellos are usually somewhat longer.

49. Russell Stinson, *J. S. Bach's Great Eighteen Organ Chorales* (New York: Oxford University Press, 2001), 21; Jean-Claude Zehnder, "Giuseppe Torelli und Johann Sebastian Bach: Zu Bachs Weimarer Konzertform," *Bach-Jahrbuch* 77 (1991): 35. The first section of BWV 655 (mm. 1–51), which both writers describe in terms of a concerto, could be viewed with equal justice as an invention or sinfonia.

50. As in the "Ritournello" that precedes the soprano solo "Ein Mensch" in Telemann's early *Trauer-Actus* (TWV 1:38), *Ach wie nichtig* (seen in the sole source, Dl Mus. ms. 2392-E-551). Although unrelated to the soprano solo except by key and meter, the passage is apparently to be repeated afterward. Heinichen's early German cantatas incorporate similar forms, as in *Es naheten aber zu Jesu* (preserved in Dl Mus. ms. 2398-E-502), in which da capo (or quasi da capo) arias for tenor and bass stand alongside strophic lieder for soprano and alto. In the autograph score of BWV 68, Bach placed the word *Ritornello*, apparently in the older sense of an instrumental refrain, at the point where he incorporated the one-movement sinfonia BWV 1040 into the end of the aria "Mein gläubiges Herze" (Zehnder, "Giuseppe Torelli und Johann Sebastian Bach," 73).

by Pisendel whose concluding Vivace opens with a tutti passage of two and a quarter measures, limited to unison arpeggiation of the tonic triad.[51] Whether such passages were understood at the time as ritornellos—that is, as analogous to the opening instrumental passage of an aria—is of course unclear.

Ritornello Design in Telemann's Instrumental Works

Clearer instances of ritornello form in the modern sense do occur in many instrumental works from the first quarter of the century. Typical is the first quick movement of Telemann's Concerto for two Violins, Viola, and Continuo in D Minor (TWV 43:d2).[52] Telemann's works are particularly relevant to our discussion; not only was he among the most prolific and widely admired composers of instrumental music in Germany, but he is the chief composer explicitly mentioned by Scheibe, even if no specific works are named. Although dates of composition for many of his works remain uncertain, a chronology emerging through the work of Zohn and others makes it clear that Telemann's approach to such parameters as form and scoring was evolving during the first two decades of the century and was hardly as rigid as Scheibe's categories imply.[53]

The second movement of TWV 43:d2 opens with a substantial passage for the full ensemble, in which all parts participate in the motivic work. After a cadence in the tonic, there follows an episode in which the two violins exchange new, somewhat more lively leaping and running figuration, leading to a partial restatement of the opening section in the relative major. The process repeats itself two or three more times. One of the work's two manuscript sources designates it a concerto, leaving no question that it was regarded as such by at least one reliable eighteenth-century witness, in this case none less than the composer Christoph Graupner.[54]

The same might be said for each of the concertos in Telemann's *Six concerts et six suites* (Hamburg, 1734), which are playable both as trios with continuo and as duos for flute and obbligato keyboard. *Concert 5* in B minor (TWV 42:h1) has become something

51. This work is preserved in Dl Mus. ms. 2421-O-6,1.

52. Modern edition in Telemann: Musikalische Werke, 28:23–29. A later version appears as *Sonata VI* in the *Quatrième livre de quatuors* attributed to Telemann (Paris, after 1752). The original bears the title *Concerto* in only one of its two manuscript sources; see Zohn, "The Ensemble Sonatas," 446, table 5.2.

53. Steven Zohn provides dates for a large number of manuscript sources in "Music Paper at the Dresden Court and the Chronology of Telemann's Instrumental Music," in *Puzzles in Paper: Concepts in Historical Watermarks*, ed. Daniel W. Mosser et al. (New Castle, Del.: Oak Knoll Press, 2000), 125–68. Dates are taken from this publication unless another source is cited. I am grateful to Steven Zohn for providing me with a copy of his essay.

54. Zohn, "The Ensemble Sonatas," speaks of this movement as a sort of double concerto (with two solo violin parts).

of an archetype for the *Sonate auf Concertenart*, having served as an example in analyses by Swack, Zohn, and Dreyfus (see Example 3).[55] Dreyfus finds that here "the identities of Telemann's ritornellos and episodes are . . . too close for comfort"—that is, they are insufficiently distinct in style. But this could not be said of many other examples by the composer, including the fourth movement of *Concert 6* (TWV 42:a2) from the same set, which ingeniously combines elements of fugue, ritornello design, and *Sonata mit zwei Themata*. In most cases, however, any apparent distinction between tutti and solo roles for two upper parts dissolves in the course of a given movement.[56] What, then, justified the generic identification as *Concert*?[57]

The presence of one quasi-ritornello form within each of these works—or within the earlier concerto TWV 43:d2—seems a relatively weak distinguishing feature when the complete four-movement design of each is taken into consideration. The overall design and style are not otherwise very different from those of some of Telemann's other concertos and sonatas. For example, in the early quartet TWV 43:G5, the second movement is not a ritornello form but a so-called concertante fugue with soloistic episodes. Its last movement employs some of the phraseology of a ritornello form, including an opening tutti followed by exchanges of material between the two violins, as occurs in some concerto movements, but it is a sonata form (i.e., a large rounded binary form).[58] The equally early TWV 43:A4 lacks any clearly articulated ritornello-form movement, although the second movement does include a lengthy solo for the first violin (mm. 37–54). The second movement also contains recurring tutti passages that are articulated like ritornello fragments in other works, even though they do not in fact restate the opening theme.[59]

Even works that we would identify without hesitation as concertos often fail to show typical features of the "Vivaldian" form. This may be because they are not, in

---

55. Swack, "On the Origins," 387–89; Zohn, "The Ensemble Sonatas," 474–75; and Dreyfus, *Bach and the Patterns of Invention*, 112–16.

56. As Swack argues in the case of the first movement of Telemann's B-minor *Concert* ("On the Origins," 387–89). Zohn and Dreyfus both analyze the latter, revealing substantially different views of what constitutes a "ritornello formation" (Dreyfus's term, *Bach and the Patterns of Invention*, 115, table 4.2; cf. Zohn, "The Ensemble Sonatas," 474–75).

57. There seems no reason to suppose that the French word, *concert*, carried implications different from those of the Italian, *concerto*.

58. TWV 43:G5 is designated a concerto in *Telemann: Musikalische Werke*, 28, which reportedly is based on the Dresden parts (Dl Mus. ms. 2392-Q-3). But the only title present in the latter is the faulty designation *Trio* on the so-called *Kapelle-Umschlag*, which contains two sets of parts, one comprising multiple doublets of all but the viola (2 x vn. 1, 2 x vn., va., 2 x "Basso," 2 x "Bassono"). Zohn dates the earlier set to "ca. 1710–20."

59. TWV 43:A4 was consulted in *Telemann: Musikalische Werke*, 28; Zohn dates it "ca. 1710–20."

Ex. 3. G. P. Telemann, *Concert* for Flute, Violin, and Continuo (or Flute and Cembalo) in B Minor (TWV 42:h1), from *Six concerts et six suites* (Hamburg, 1734), second mvt. (opening).

fact, "Vivaldian" concertos. In the first quick movement of the concerto TWV 52:G2 (which J. S. Bach copied around 1709), the two ripieno violins function as almost equal partners of the two *concertato* violins, supplying countersubjects to the latter's subject entries in the fugal exposition that opens the movement. There are brief episodes for the two soloists, but these are short and lyrical, not virtuoso in character. The last movement is cast in a sort of ternary form not unlike that of the first movement in Bach's Fourth Brandenburg Concerto, where the A section incorporates solo episodes yet (from the modern point of view) resembles a large ritornello. Here, as in the fugue, the *concertato* parts are doubled by *ripieni* only in portions of those tutti sections that seem to function like ritornellos. Perhaps this feature, together with the generally outgoing, virtuoso style of the tuttis (in contrast to the "solo" episodes), was sufficient to mark the piece as a concerto. Yet it is not very different in formal conception from the Sonata in F for five parts (TWV 44:11),[60] which, however, employs more restrained violin writing and more consistently contrapuntal textures.

TWV 52:G2 is one of the many works designated as both concertos and sonatas to include a so-called *concertante* fugue. Although the parallels to ritornello form in such movements are sometimes obvious (at least to us), many movements that have been designated *concertante* fugues are to some degree ambiguous. For instance, the second movement (Allegro) of the quartet TWV 43:A6 for two violins, viola, and continuo, is a double fugue; the viola serves as an equal partner in the opening exposition, but in the following episode, only the two violins exchange figuration antiphonally. This passage might be considered a solo episode[61] except that the soloistic figuration appears only here and in one brief passage toward the end—insufficient, it would seem, for the passage to have the same effect as a solo episode in a concerto. Moreover, this is one of numerous works for which Pisendel had numerous doublets copied at Dresden, and in this version all of the violins share the soloistic passagework, doubled as well by oboes (which play it in somewhat simplified form).[62] Evidently Pisendel, a virtuoso violinist who would certainly have recognized a potential concerto solo when he saw one, saw no reason to assign the episodes to reduced forces.

Ritornello Design in Bach's Instrumental Works

When we turn to Bach's works, initial impressions of ritornello form are similarly open to qualification. In chamber works such as the A-Major Sonata (BWV 1032) (see Example 2), or even in the Second Brandenburg Concerto,[63] the assignment of each part to a

---

60. Quantz, in his copies of the parts (Dl Mus. ms. 2392-14a), assigns the latter to strings; they are unspecified in the score copied in part by Pisendel (Dl Mus. ms. 2392-Q-14). Incidentally, the first allegro treats in five-part stretto a fugue subject virtually identical to that of Bach's Fughetta (BWV 901/1) in the same key (better known in its revised version as the Fugue in A in the *Well-Tempered Clavier* II).

61. Zohn, "The Ensemble Sonatas," 496n68, calls this movement a "concertante fugue."

62. The parts, in Dl Mus. ms. 2392-N-6a and 2392-N-6b, bear the title *Sinfonia*.

63. Originally a quintet for four melody instruments and continuo, according to the convincing argument of Klaus Hofmann, "Zur Fassungsgeschichte des 2. Brandenburgische Konzerts," in BOW, 185–92.

tutti or a solo role emerges as arbitrary after the opening passages. Analysis in terms of ritornello and solo sections gradually becomes untenable as one proceeds through each quick movement. Thus, in the first movement of the A-Major Sonata, mm. 25–35 constitute an elaborated repeat of the opening ritornello, transposed to the dominant and rescored. Yet within the extant fragment of the movement, there is no subsequent restatement of a coherent ritornello, and even the one at m. 25 is substantially altered.[64] Similarly, in the opening Vivace movement of the C-Minor Organ Sonata (BWV 526), the distinction between ritornello ("tutti") and episode ("solo") breaks down after the third ritornello (mm. 31–38). In the ensuing passage, motivic material from both the opening ritornello and elsewhere is used in free *Fortspinnung*, and there are no firmly articulated statements of either the ritornello theme or of the episode theme previously introduced fugally at m. 8b.[65] The eventual restatement of a sequential passage from the ritornello in mm. 61–62 thus has no clear articulatory significance. It confirms the return to the tonic key area that has occurred by this point, but it carries none of the force of a closing ritornello or tutti passage in a solo concerto.

More fundamental than the supposed tutti or solo character of any instrumental part may be the mere presence of some sort of contrast between the types of material associated with each of the upper parts, at least in their initial entries. Thus, as Swack has observed, in the A-Major Sonata (BWV 1032) (See Example 2), the flute enters with a contrasting lyrical theme, and nowhere in the surviving fragment does this part play the virtuoso passagework characteristic of the mature solo concerto.[66] That this was a normal procedure emerges from such instances as the Graun sonata (Example 1), in which the flute entrance is marked Cantabile, and from the first movements of the doubtful sonatas for flute and cembalo BWV 1020 and 1031.[67] In some works, such as

---

64. The sole independent source of Bach's BWV 1032 is an autograph (P 612) in which the first movement is written in the space remaining beneath the systems occupied by the Concerto for Two Cembali, Strings, and Continuo in C Minor (BWV 1062). The removal of approximately forty-six measures of the first movement of the flute sonata from the bottoms of the later pages of the manuscript has left an irretrievable lacuna. See the facsimile in *Johann Sebastian Bach: Konzert c-moll für zwei Cembali und Streichorchester* BWV 1062 / Sonate A-dur für Flöte und Cembalo BWV 1032, ed. Hans-Joachim Schulze, *Documenta musicologica, Zweite Reihe: Handschriften-Faksimiles* 10 (Kassel: Bärenreiter, 1980).

65. Cf. Williams (*The Organ Music*, 1:26): elements of the ritornello of BWV 526/1 "could follow each other in various orders"; he cites the instance in which "the passage built on sequential trills" leads first to passage "B" (m. 22) and later to "A" (mm. 70–71).

66. Swack, "On the Origins," 404–5.

67. Other examples occur in Telemann's quartet sonatas or concertos TWV 43:g2, 43:G12, and 43:A4. Mary Oleskiewicz, "Quantz and the Flute at Dresden: His Instruments, His Repertory, and Their Significance for the *Versuch* and the Bach Circle" (Ph.D. diss., Duke University, 1998), 245, finds that in about a quarter of Quantz's concerto movements. the flute enters with material "more

the Graun sonata in A (Example 1), the original dichotomy between the two melody instruments is retained throughout the movement; the violin never plays the flute's new theme, and the flute plays only material from the later portions of the violin's opening (ritornello) passage. Bach allows a greater amount of interplay in most such movements, but in the extant portion of BWV 1032/1, as in Wendt 8, the harpsichord never plays the flute's opening gesture.

Perhaps in this movement Bach departed from the principle of equal or fully interchangeable upper voices. A precedent occurs in the Concerto for Two Cembali (BWV 1060), where the two soloists have distinctly different types of material. This differentiation provides the basis for the common assumption that the work was originally scored for two contrasting solo instruments, namely, oboe and violin.[68] One might suppose a similar differentiation of the upper voices in the first movement of BWV 1032. On the other hand, the absence of any such differentiation in the original version of the movement might be why Bach, if it was he, excised a portion of the existing manuscript, perhaps intending to replace it with a new version. The principle of voice exchange does appear to be introduced in m. 62, immediately after which the fragment breaks off.

Scheibe's account of the *Sonate auf Concertenart* does not specifically call for passagework in the leading part, unless one understands this in his reference to *kräuselnde* and *verändernde Sätze*. He notes only the possibility of the soloists introducing new material after the initial ritornello. But rather than speaking in terms derived from the concerto (or the aria), one might describe such a work as a dialogue of equal partners that may eventually join in the presentation of material introduced by the one or the other. As Williams argues, even in a work such as the first movement of the G-Major Organ Sonata (BWV 530), which presents the "clearest" instance in the organ sonatas of "a concerto-like arrangement with quasi-tutti and solo [passages,] . . . this tutti/solo structure is no more than a framework invoked now and then." Williams adds that "formal ambiguities are typical of forms transferred from one medium (concerto) to another (organ sonata)."[69] But it remains possible that the version of ritornello form found in BWV 1032/1 and other obbligato–keyboard works of Bach originated entirely within the tradition of the instrumental duo with continuo accompaniment.

This is not to deny the obvious points in common between concerto and sonata

---

lyrical than the ritornello" but that the solo episodes of quick movements usually still proceed to virtuoso writing.

68. See the reconstruction in Wilfried Fischer, ed., NBA VII/7 (*Verschollene Solokonzerte in Rekonstruktion*), which is based on previous reconstructions by Max Schneider and Max Seiffert (according to Fischer, NBA VII/7, KB, 104).

69. *The Organ Music*, 33–34.

movements that share some sort of antithesis between the first two main formal sections. By 1720 or so, such an antithesis was certainly an expected feature in the quick movements of a concerto, even in movements whose overall form was more like that of a sonata. Binary form is not today associated with the concerto, and indeed it is rare in works composed after 1725 or so. But it is by no means unusual before then, as evidenced by the final movements of the concerto TWV 43:A4, Marcello's E-Minor Concerto, op. 1 no. 2 (Venice, 1708), or the two quick movements of a Heinichen *Concerto a 6* in B.[70] In each case, the two halves of the binary form open and close with tutti passages, separated by modulating solo passages. This creates a phraseology resembling that of ritornello form and, together with the presence of at least a few phrases of vigorous passagework (whether or not for solo parts), might have made such movements seem appropriate to a concerto. Vivaldi nevertheless replaced such movements with through-composed forms in two of the concertos that Bach transcribed for keyboard,[71] implying that binary-form movements were coming to be viewed in Venice as inappropriate to concertos at a time when they remained common elements of the genre in other places. Simultaneously, what we call ritornello forms must only then have been emerging as normal or customary elements of concerto movements becoming genre markers through a gradual process.

Scoring and Instrumentation

Orchestral scoring has been taken as another marker of the concerto. But the modern notion of the concerto as an orchestral genre, that is, one in which the ripieno parts are doubled, is inconsistently documented before 1750 or so. Although multiple doublets for ripieno parts exist for many Dresden concertos,[72] surviving sets of parts for concertos from the Bach circle rarely include duplicate parts intended for a single performance. Peter Holman and Richard Maunder have shown to what degree this is true in other parts of Europe, as well.[73] The expansion of what would now be regarded

---

70. Autograph score in Dl Mus. ms. 2398-O-5.

71. Concertos RV 316a and RV 381, transcribed by Bach (presumably from manuscript versions) as BWV 975 and 980. Later versions without binary-form movements were published in Vivaldi's op. 4 (Amsterdam, ca. 1714). Mary Oleskiewicz ("Quantz and the Flute at Dresden," 243–57) points out that the lively sort of exchange particularly characteristic of this sort of concerto movement is also found in numerous binary-form sonata movements that might therefore have been regarded as *concertenartig*.

72. See Oleskiewicz, "Quantz and the Flute at Dresden," 263–72. Swack, "On the Origins," 385–87, cites an instance of a Telemann *Concerto à 3* for which a Darmstadt set of manuscript parts includes several *Doubletten*.

73. Peter Homan and Richard Maunder, "The Accompaniment of Concertos in 18th-Century England," *Early Music* 29 (2000): 637–50.

as chamber works through added ripieno parts was not necessarily accompanied by changes in title. Hence one must wonder whether concertos were identified by their resemblance to pieces more specifically associated with large ensembles, such as the sinfonias of contemporary Italian operas and oratorios.

That the term *concerto* had nothing to do with instrumentation, at least at Dresden, is confirmed by the Dresden practice of doubling the parts of trio and quartet sonatas, evidently for performances at the court church. Although truncating most pieces so that they include only the first two movements (which seem always to comprise a slow introduction followed by a fugue), Pisendel's arrangements often retain the original title (typically *Sonata*). And, as in the so-called *concertante* fugue of TWV 43:A6, where we might expect to find certain "soloistic" episodes assigned to soloists, all parts remain identical: Pisendel introduced no distinction between ripieno and *concertato* parts.[74] Mary Oleskiewicz has argued that "the number of players per part in Dresden was determined primarily by (1) the style of the music and (2) the performing venue"—that is, not by title or what we would presume to be the genre designation.[75] Hence, as late as 1750 the terms *concerto* and *sonata* continued to lack any implications for "orchestral" as opposed to "chamber" scoring, at least for Pisendel.

Other "Gestures" as Markers

Two trios by Telemann copied by the Dresden court composer Ristori under the title *Concerto a tre* incorporate several brief unison or octave passages, gestures that occur consistently in Italian orchestral music, but apart from that there is nothing orchestral about these pieces.[76] The same seems to be true of Telemann's 1734 *Concerts* and, in general, of the trios and quartets mentioned previously. The occasional parallels to certifiably orchestral music are so few and far between that they seem hardly sufficient to account for a generic assignment. Similar strictures apply to Telemann's *Concerto alla polonese* for two violins, viola, and continuo (TWV 43:G7), in which the occasional passages in octaves (not to mention ritornellos that enter in surprise keys without transition) seem to reflect imitation of vernacular improvised music making,

74. In addition to TWV 43:A6, examples examined here include movements in the concerto TWV 43: Es 1 (Dl Mus. ms. 2392-N-12), the trios TWV 42:F11 and 42:A11 (both in Dl Mus. ms. 2392-N-7), the sonata TWV 42:g13 (Dl Mus. ms. 2392-Q-50), and the trio TWV 43:G5 (Dl Mus. ms. Q-3). Titles are from the Dresden parts or their wrappers; the latter date from the second half of the eighteenth century and thus are of little consequence for our present purposes.

75. "Quantz and the Flute at Dresden," 270.

76. Dl Mus. mss. 2392–Q-31 (TWV 42:D15) and 2392–Q-37 (TWV 42:e7). Both sources are in oblong format (22 x 31cm); neither contains doublets. A third Ristori copy of the trio TWV 43:A9 (illustrated in Example 6 below), also entitled *Concerto* and in the same format, lacks even these possible concerto "markers."

not Italian orchestral music.[77] Here the title, if it has any significance at all, might be ironic or satirical.

Among other "markers" proposed as concerto identifiers are several that might more logically be connected to vocal music. Apart from the ritornello itself, these include instrumental imitations of recitative and aria styles. Instrumental recitative occurs famously in the slow movement of Vivaldi's "Grosso Mogul" concerto (RV 208) (transcribed by Bach as BWV 594 and seemingly imitated by him in the Chromatic Fantasia [BWV 903/1]). But it also occurs in Francesco Antonio Bonporti's *Invenzioni da camera* for violin and continuo, op. 10 (Bologna, 1712), as well as in a flute sonata now considered an early work of Handel.[78] Modern commentators have even seen imitations of recitative in much older works, including keyboard pieces by Fresco-baldi and Kuhnau and chamber sonatas of Buxtehude. Hence there is little reason for associating recitative-like features in such works as the sonata *a quattro* (TWV 43:F1) or the concerto TWV 43:D4 specifically with the Italian concerto style. If not directly inspired by the actual vocal form, these works might well reflect an already well-established tradition of instrumental recitative.

If the vocal derivation of these quasi-recitative movements is self-evident, the same must hold for aria-like movements in instrumental works. To be sure, as soon as instrumental composers began to imitate vocal gestures, these would have become part of the vocabulary of instrumental music, as well. For example, it is easy to imagine a vocal inspiration for the aria-like adagios of certain Vivaldi concertos in which the soloist is accompanied by continuo alone (or by homophonic ripieno parts). In one such work attributed to Vivaldi, the Concerto for Flute, Violin, and Continuo in D Major (RV 84), the singing character of the principal part is made explicit by the word *cantabile*—a term also found in the Graun trio illustrated in Example 1.[79] But German composers might have composed similar movements as much in emulation of Vivaldi's concertos as in direct imitation of vocal writing. Thus florid solos in the third movement (Largo) of Telemann's *Concert 1* of 1734 are framed by opening and closing passages for the tutti; this design resembles less an aria than the slow movement in works such as Vivaldi's D-Major Concerto, op. 3 no. 9 (RV 230).

In general, however, the aria was such a fixture in sacred as well as secular music throughout the eighteenth century that it is difficult to believe that it would not have

---

77. Seen in Dl Mus. ms. 2392-Q-2; two modern editions were unavailable.

78. HWV 58; see Oleskiewicz, "Quantz and the Flute at Dresden," 475–76.

79. In some cases, the word *cantabile* may have served simply to indicate to the player the leading character of his part, as when Bach used the same indication in the last movement of the Fifth Brandenburg Concerto. RV 84 is anonymous in its only source, a Dresden manuscript copy. I am grateful to Mary Oleskiewicz for the information that its wrapper, dating from the later eighteenth century, groups it with items attributed to Vivaldi.

remained a direct model for instrumental imitations. In addition to furnishing the fundamental idea of ritornello form, arias furnished models for general styles or types of both ritornello and solo.[80] Many local gestures in instrumental music might also be associated with the aria. For example, at the initial "solo" entry in the first movement of Bach's G-Minor Gamba Sonata (BWV 1029), the long-held note sustained by a trill in the right hand of the cembalo part is reminiscent of certain types of aria.[81] The fugal manner in which the closing theme of the ritornello is later developed (mm. 26–29) may be reminiscent of the trio sonata or even the double or "group" concerto, but it is equally characteristic of the vocal duet.[82] Indeed, when one considers the centrality of vocal music in Bach's output, and in Baroque music as a whole, it seems somewhat arbitrary to relate such gestures primarily to instrumental genres. Vocal music, particularly opera seria, is at least as plausible as the source of models and markers that eventually came to be associated with the concerto. But each potential element must, like ritornello form, have had a separate history that only gradually became a marker for one genre or another.

Some Alternatives

How might my proposal alter our understanding of Bach's music and his development as a composer? I have two broad suggestions:

REEVALUATING THE RITORNELLO

First, recent studies of the concerto and its relationships to other genres may have overstated the importance of the ritornello, which, as noted in preceding paragraphs, did not in fact constitute the "essence" of the late Baroque concerto, at least for Scheibe.[83] As a corollary, certain formal principles and compositional devices currently associated with concerto movements in ritornello form may in fact have a more general significance. For example, it has become fashionable to understand the so-called

---

80. Cf. the unison minor-key ritornello of many "rage" arias or the lyrical entry of the soloist after a lively orchestral tutti, as in Riccardo Broschi's insert aria "Son qual navi" for Hasse's *Artaserse*, rendered familiar through its presentation in Gérard Corbiau's 1995 film *Farinelli il castrato*.

81. Particularly relevant here are the examples from works by Handel, Hasse, Zelenka, and others discussed in Oleskiewicz, "Quantz and the Flute at Dresden," 174–89 and 290–329.

82. The typical trio-sonata movement opening with a statement of the theme by one instrument and its repetition at the fifth above by another has a distinct parallel in the type of duet exemplified by the famous "Se mai più sarò geloso" from Hasse's opera *Cleofide*, first performed at Dresden in 1731 with Bach in attendance.

83. Nor was the ritornello paramount for later theorists such as Heinrich Christoph Koch, a point long ago established by Jane Stevens, "An Eighteenth-Century Description."

"Vivaldian ritornello" as a tripartite structure comprised of *Vordersatz*, *Fortspinnung*, and *Epilog*. This is to assign such ritornellos to Wilhelm Fischer's *Fortspinnungstypus*, one of two basic categories of phrase structure Fischer discerned in eighteenth-century instrumental music.[84] Many Italianate ritornellos, however, are constituted simply of antecedent and consequent, the latter incorporating both *Fortspinnung* and *Epilog*.[85] This is particularly clear where the *Epilog* is a brief cadential formula and not a distinct phrase.[86]

This casts into doubt the idea that an "ideal ritornello" belonging to Fischer's *Fortspinnungstypus* lies at the root of many late Baroque movements whose actual ritornellos take alternate forms. Among these is the Vivace of Bach's G-Minor Gamba Sonata (BWV 1029), of which it has been asserted that "conventional Bachian features include an ideal ritornello that appears nowhere in the movement intact."[87] The concept resembles the Schenkerian *Ursatz* in being a normative structure that is posited as underlying actual music. As such it is less a verifiable claim about Bach's compositional process (or "conventions") than an argument for hearing his ritornellos as elaborations or variations of the scheme represented by Fischer's *Fortspinnungstypus*. Not all ritornellos follow that scheme, however. The opening ritornello in the first movement of the Second Brandenburg Concerto is more readily analyzed as an instance of Fischer's *Liedtypus*—the alternative model consisting essentially of antecedent and consequent. To be sure, the subsequent expansion of this ritornello in the course of the movement includes the interpolation of the same sequential *Fortspinnung* already present in the opening ritornellos in other works.

In any case, the *Fortspinnungstypus* has no special connection with the concerto ritornello. As Fischer's original article made clear, much the same type of tripartite structure can be found in sonata movements and other late Baroque instrumental works. Indeed, Zehnder uses Fischer's principle as a model for analyzing concerto episodes.[88] In short, the three parts of the *Fortspinnungstypus* are not limited to ritornello segments in concerto movements. As Fischer argued, they are fundamental elements

---

84. Fischer's terminology, part of a general theory of eighteenth-century form, appears in his "Zur Entwicklungsgeschichte des Wiener klassischen Stils," *Studien zur Musikwissenschaft* 3 (1915): 24–84; Dreyfus adopted it for the analysis of concertos in "J. S. Bach's Concerto Ritornellos and the Question of Invention," *Musical Quarterly* 71 (1985): 327–58, subsequently incorporated (in part) into *Bach and the Patterns of Invention*, 59–102.

85. See Butler, "J. S. Bach's Reception," 22n12.

86. As in the ritornello from Vivaldi's *Suonata* RV 779 (see Swack, "On the Origins," 377).

87. Dreyfus, *Bach and the Patterns of Invention*, 109.

88. Zehnder, "Giuseppe Torelli und Johann Sebastian Bach," 41.

of eighteenth-century formal design, even if few today would follow him in relating the Classical sonata-allegro directly to a ternary type of Baroque ritornello.

The segments of a ritornello that falls into Fischer's *Fortspinnungstypus* perform what have been described as certain structural "functions."[89] But these, too, are hardly unique to concerto ritornellos. As already alluded to, they are none other than the basic articulatory functions of a large portion of the early eighteenth-century repertory: procedures whose semiotic role is to differentiate particular segments of typical late Baroque designs, such as rounded binary dance movements and through-composed ternary and rondo-like forms.[90] Thus Fischer's *Vordersatz* corresponds to a type of thematic statement that initiates a major formal section and establishes a tonality or confirms one previously established. His *Fortspinnung* is a type of bridge passage, most frequently a sequence or series of such phrases. His *Epilog* is a type of closing passage that articulates the end of a major section. Each of these functions can be served by any number of passages in a given movement, including components of both ritornellos and solo episodes. Indeed, the presence of multiple passages serving similar functions is what makes possible the kaleidoscopic reordering of phrase segments in the course of certain early eighteenth-century movements, including Bach's. The functions of these passages are not limited to the articulation of a movement's large-scale modulatory design. For instance, the initiating function of the opening phrase of a ritornello—its *Vordersatz*—is served by gestures such as the forceful outlining of a tonic triad that acquired, by convention, the status of "opening" figures in many contexts. Such gestures could even be used meaningfully in isolation, as in brief orchestral statements within accompanied recitative. Nevertheless, it is in the articulation of large, tonally rounded designs that these functions are of special importance, as they made possible the emergence of compositions based on such designs at the start of the eighteenth century.

That the "ritornello functions" as hitherto defined are special cases of more general procedures becomes clear when one examines the seemingly irregular or transitional types of concerto movements that are especially prevalent during the first two decades of the eighteenth century—binary-form movements, as well as those with unusually short ritornellos, which to us seem to employ the phraseology of the solo concerto

89. Dreyfus, *Bach and the Patterns of Invention*, 60–62. These functions are not to be confused with certain ones also designated by Dreyfus in earlier publications as "ritornello functions" and labeled in capital letters, e.g., "MODESWITCH." The latter are not structural functions but operations performed on segments of the "ideal ritornello," as when the mode is switched from major to minor. Despite the novel labeling, these would seem to constitute nothing other than the regular procedures of tonal counterpoint.

90. The underlying formal model is the type of early eighteenth-century sonata form I delineated in *The Instrumental Music of C. P. E. Bach* (Ann Arbor, Mich.: UMI Research Press, 1984), 100–102.

without adopting all of the familiar aspects of its form. Here the "ritornello" or tutti passages tend to perform the functions of initiation and closing, whereas the "solos," which may be quite brief and may contain lyrical passages, not virtuoso figuration, fill the role of modulating *Fortspinnung*. These examples seem to date from precisely the period in which Bach was forming his approach to writing music for instrumental ensembles, roughly, his Weimar years (1708–17). This suggests that his own heterogeneous approach to form in such works as the Brandenburg Concertos was the result not of deliberate genre blending but rather of simply following procedures that he had found in models that were available to him and, of course, developing them in his own unusually rigorous and original ways.

In textbook ritornello form, the melodic and rhythmic elements that ordinarily mark each of these functions are reinforced by scoring. For example, entries of the opening theme or *Vordersatz* tend also to be marked by the entry of the ripieno instruments, thus strengthening the initiating function of the first phrase of the ritornello. But in the absence of ripieno parts, the marking of this phrase lacks such reinforcement, hence weakening the formal functioning of the passage or rendering it ambiguous. Such ambiguity can arise in a so-called *Sonate auf Concertenart* if it becomes unclear which of the contrasting themes associated with the upper parts serves to announce or articulate major structural divisions. The bifurcated scoring of such a work can complicate the semiotics of the formal design, modifying the articulatory power or structural functions of the principal thematic ideas. In some works, the result may be to blur distinctions between different thematic ideas over the course of a movement as "solo" or episodic phrases become equivalent in articulatory force to statements of the opening theme. Such is arguably the case in the first movement of BWV 1029 and in some of the Brandenburg Concertos, where, for all the ingenuity of Bach's permutational counterpoint and the seamless connecting of sections, there is an arbitrariness in the ordering of thematic passages except at those few points where the opening ritornello phrase is restated by the melody parts in unison.

The rapid development of this semiotic system during the first two decades of the eighteenth century, particularly but by no means exclusively in the Venetian concerto, was a crucial element in the emergence of late Baroque style. Within Bach's music, its adoption in the preludes from the English Suites and some of the organ preludes distinguishes these from earlier compositions in similar genres. The development of the three structural functions underlying Fischer's *Fortspinnungstypus* around 1700 was essential for the types of large-scale formal structures that we take for granted in eighteenth-century music, above all, Bach's. These presuppose the use of modulation articulated by transposed recurrences of one or more thematic ideas—as the basis for the formal designs of large movements, not only in concertos, but in sonatas, suites, fugues, and the like.

Ritornello forms, in which a single recurring thematic passage articulates each new modulation, are an important example of such a design, but they are far from unique. Their importance lies in the fact that in them the articulatory power of the recurring theme is strengthened by the principle of alternation, which might be considered yet another type of structural function. We are most familiar with this function in the alternation of soloist and full ensemble in a concerto movement, but the same function is served by the entry of one or more vocal soloists in an aria, by that of a cantus firmus phrase after an interlude in a chorale fantasia, or, more generally, by the introduction of new or contrasting material at the beginning of any distinctly articulated section. The fact that composers shortly after 1700 adopted essentially the same formal pattern for compositions belonging to distinct genres—aria, chorale, concerto movement—points to the power of these new functions. (It also suggests that the stylistic break conventionally placed around 1750 should be pushed back fifty years or so, as Classical sonata-allegro form is really a special case of the more general formal design here described, but that is another matter.)

The unusually rigorous application of this principle in Bach's keyboard works and sonatas, together with the well-known testimony that he learned to "think musically" through study of Vivaldi's concertos, has encouraged the impression that many of his compositions were directly modeled after concertos.[91] This might well reflect a perception that was prevalent even in Bach's own household. But no witness points to formal design as the particular element that Bach learned from Vivaldi. And in considering the relationships between Vivaldi's concertos and various German works of the teens and early 1720s, we may be projecting current postmodernist ideals onto the eighteenth-century composers of such movements in supposing that the latter constitute deliberate interweavings of concerto- and sonata-like features.

The tutti–solo alternation of many concerto allegros is a particularly effective way of serving the "alternation" function. Nevertheless, this is merely a special case of a dialoguing, or, as Williams has described it, a "duologuing" principle.[92] A dialectic involving thematic material, expressive character, instrumental color, and harmonic and melodic rhythm lies at the core of innumerable eighteenth-century instrumental pieces, not just concerto movements in ritornello form. This is not, of course, the dialectic of Classical sonata-allegro form but rather one that involves the setting up

---

91. See Christoph Wolff, "Vivaldi's Compositional Art, Bach, and the Process of 'Musical Thinking,'" in *Johann Sebastian Bach: Essays on His Life and Music* (Cambridge, Mass.: Harvard University Press, 1991), 72–83.

92. In the first edition of *The Organ Music of J. S. Bach*, 3 vols. (Cambridge: Cambridge University Press, 1980–84), 1:89fn, Williams explained the duologue as "a 'dramatic piece with two actors', rather than 'dialogue', 'conversation in general', i.e.[,] with more than two."

of more local and immediate oppositions between distinct types of musical ideas. An extreme instance occurs in C. P. E. Bach's so-called *Programm-Trio* of 1749, W. 161/1 (H. 579), in which the two upper parts, each with its own sharply contrasting material, explicitly represent two personified characters (Example 4).[93] How other, less extreme, dialoguing works might have been understood is suggested by the rubric attached to the work shown in Example 5. The identification of the latter in two sources as a *Sonata con 2. Themata* presumably refers to the use in the first movement of distinct themes for the initial entries of the upper parts. This expression, not *Sonate auf Concertenart*, is in fact the only one applied in eighteenth-century sources to specific pieces of the type to which commentators have applied Scheibe's term.[94]

Dialectical oppositions of all sorts are a particularly common feature in the opening passages of movements from Telemann's instrumental works. These include not only the now-paradigmatic dialectic of tutti and solo in concertos, but oppositions between two sonorities (instruments or instrumental groups), two thematic ideas, or two styles of melodic or rhythmic writing. It would appear that Telemann throughout his career was fascinated by the possibility of setting up such a dialectic at the outset of a movement, then working it out through continued simple alternation, gradual assimilation, or polyphonic combination of two ideas in double counterpoint. A mature instance of this technique occurs in the *Concert 5* in B minor (Example 3). But the technique employed there is a development of the simpler and more short-winded dialectic employed in the earlier work shown in Example 6.[95] Suggestions for such a

---

93. Emanuel Bach spelled out the significance of each phrase in the preface to his *Zwey Trio* (Nürnberg, 1751). The sonata, which is the first work of the pair, can be performed either with two violins or with the right hand of the keyboard replacing the first violin.

94. Swack, "On the Origins," 405, interprets the inscription (added by a second hand to the title in Berlin, Staatsbibliothek, ms. 8284/22) as an effort to solve "the problem of genre in the sonata in the concerted manner." I see rather an allusion to the language of fugue, referring not to the presence of a "concerted" manner but to that of two contrasting themes or subjects (in place of a single subject echoed by the second part). A second copy of the same work from the collection of Sara Levy, bearing an unambiguous attribution to "Sr J[ohann] G[ottlieb] Graun Sen[ior]," has turned up in a manuscript copy, Berlin, Sing-Akademie (Bsa) SA 3699, which also contains a copy of W. 8 similarly labeled (Bsa SA 3772). Both copies bear the same reference to "two themes," assigning the second part alternatively to violin or obbligato keyboard.

95. The work illustrated in Example 6 has a conflicting attribution to the opera composer Antonio Lotti. Based on what little of the latter's instrumental music is available for comparison, the style appears to be more typical of Telemann. Comparable examples abound in Telemann's early instrumental works. For example, the Concerto for Two Recorders, Two Oboes, Two Violins, and Continuo in F Major (TWV 44:41) (preserved in Dl Mus. ms. 2392-O-28) expands the principle of antiphony from two individual parts to three *pairs* of like instruments. In the second movement (*Vivace*) the violin pair works in opposition to the two woodwind pairs, having different, more lively material.

Ex. 4. C. P. E. Bach, Sonata for Two Violins and Continuo in C Minor (W. 161/1
[H. 579]), from *Zwey Trio* (Nürnberg, 1751), first mvt. (opening).

Ex. 5. C. H. Graun, *Sonata a tre in G# con 2. themata* (Wendt 78), first mvt. (opening).

Ex. 6. G. P. Telemann, Sonata for Flute, Oboe d'Amore (or Violin), and Continuo in A Major (TWV 42:A9), first mvt. (opening).

dialectical approach to composition might have been found in polychoral writing (still flourishing in both vocal and instrumental music at the turn of the century), dialogue passages in opera and cantata, and ballet movements that alternate between contrasting dance types.

BACH'S USE OF ALTERNATIVE SCHEMES

If Bach's contemporaries were busy exploring the possibilities of all sorts of "duologuing" designs in both instrumental and vocal music at precisely the time when he began composing, shortly after 1700, then what we call the Vivaldian concerto was just one manifestation of the process. My second suggestion, therefore, is that we seek to understand more clearly how Bach learned the principles involved and how their application in his music differs from that of his contemporaries. For instance, a number of early keyboard movements have rondo-like designs whose modulating scheme is articulated by a returning thematic idea. Among these are the one-movement Sonata in A Minor (BWV 967) and several movements from the *manualiter* toccatas.[96] Fugal works sometimes take similar forms, notably the Capriccio (BWV 993) and several others in which a lengthy subject alternates with long episodes composed of virtuoso passagework.

It is easy to understand such works by analogy to the solo concerto.[97] But by explaining their forms through the more general principle of alternation, it is possible to avoid the not very convincing claim that these works significantly resemble concertos. On the other hand, even when Bach explicitly took up the new Venetian genre, like Heinichen and others, he sometimes employed ritornellos and other now-familiar gestures in ways that do not yet correspond fully with the textbook ritornello form. Thus Bach combined tutti–solo alternations with bipartite designs in a number of movements, as in the opening allegro of the A-Minor Violin Concerto (BWV 1041), whose form is illustrated in Figure 1. The top line of the table shows the now-conventional analysis, based on recurrences of a ritornello that alternates with solo episodes. The bottom two lines show, on the other hand, that the solo episodes articulate a design comparable to what was becoming, during the second decade of the eighteenth century, the standard form for the A section in a da capo–form aria.[98]

The bipartite analysis depends on understanding the restatement of solo material at the dominant in mm. 85–88 as dividing the movement into two large sections; the

96. In a lost manuscript copy of the G-Major Toccata (BWV 916), Heinrich Nicolaus Gerber, a student of Bach, called it *Concerto seu Toccata pour le Clavecin*. But it is impossible to know whether the first word of his title referred to the quasi-ritornello design of the first movement, the three-movement form of the piece as a whole (unique among the *manualiter* toccatas), or the general character of the figuration in the first movement, which makes constant use of several motives reminiscent of the Venetian violin concerto.

97. Rondo form and fugue occur in early concertos, both, for example, occurring in different movements of the Telemann double concerto copied by J. S. Bach (TWV 52:G2). There the first quick movement is a fugue in six real parts and the fugue constitutes the whole of the movement, not merely the ritornellos (as in the last movement of BWV 1041).

98. Only gradually did the bipartite design of the A section become a consistent feature of da capo arias in German cantatas. It is absent in earlier works by, for example, Telemann and Heinichen, whose arias differ from later ones in the brevity and simplicity of their A sections (which in some cases might be considered simple refrains), lack of full integration of the ritornello (which may likewise be a simple instrumental refrain), and the writing out of the da capo in vocal and continuo parts (a sign that the convention was not yet widely understood). For instance, the bass aria "Getreu verbleiben biß in Todt" of Telemann's *Seÿ getreu biß in den Todt* (TWV 1:1284) lacks a bipartite A section, and the *Rittornello* (so designated in Dl Mus. ms. 2392-E-613) is a separate passage that echoes the opening of the vocal part. In the third movement, the alto solo "Dich lieb ich allein," the text of the A section constitutes a single verse, although its music is longer than that of the through-composed B section.

Figure 1. Analysis of Opening Movement of J. S. Bach's Concerto for Violin,
Strings and Continuo in A Minor (BWV 1041)

section:	R	S	(r)	S	R	||	
tonality:	a–e	a	a	→	C–e	||	
measure:	1	25	40	44	52	||	
recurring:		W	X	Y	Z	||	
segments:		mm.25–28	40–43	44–55	60–84	||	

section:	S	(r)	S	|	(r)	S	R
tonality:	e→	d	→	|	a	a	a
measure:	85	102	106	|	123	127	143
recurring:	W	X'		|	X	Y	Z
segments:	85–88	102–5		|	123–26	135–46	147–71

second half proceeds as a free reprise of the first.[99] Bach's particular accomplishment here was an amalgamation of dialectical structure with bilateral symmetry. Within such a movement, the alternation between tutti and solo that initially might occupy one's attention fades somewhat in relative significance, as the solo part is contrapuntally interwoven with the others and other formal principles come into play. The opening ritornello is never repeated in its complete form, and in this connection it is worth remembering that an opera-seria aria often contains a complete ritornello only at the beginning of the A section; there may not be any other ritornellos except at the end of the A section, both then being in the tonic. It is true that Vivaldi, Albinoni, and others regularly incorporated greater numbers of full or partial ritornellos in quick concerto movements by 1710 or so. But the aria, with its smaller number of ritornellos and somewhat more substantial role for the soloist, must have presented an equally influential model for Bach and others.

Similar considerations apply to the Fourth Brandenburg Concerto, whose first movement has been regarded as both a ritornello form with an unusually long first ritornello and a da capo form with a disproportionately short A section.[100] Both analyses

99. Actually, the reprise can be extended back to the ritornello material beginning in the second half of m. 59. But only at m. 85 does the entry of the soloist after a full cadence and rest constitute a sufficiently strong articulation to suggest a new beginning. This bipartite design is an example of what Joel Lester has called a "parallel structure" movement (*Bach's Works for Solo Violin: Style, Structure, Performance* [New York: Oxford University Press, 1999], 89–103). In his account, such designs resemble variation forms rather than, as here, the A section of an operatic aria containing two main statements of the first stanza of the text.

100. Butler, "The Question of Genre," 9, designates it "sonata da-capo form."

have points in their favor, but, like the broadly comparable preludes of English Suites II–VI, which might have been preliminary compositional essays for movements of this type, the movement represents an almost unique type, invented by Bach around 1713, that could not have appeared more than a few years earlier or later—not much earlier, because the solo concerto, with its principle of alternation between tuttis and solos (on the model of the virtuoso aria), had not yet been invented, and not much later, for by 1725 or so, what we now understand as through-composed ritornello form was being routinely employed in the quick movements of virtually all concertos.[101]

What Bach has done in such works is not so much to combine genres as to employ a diverse set of conventional compositional devices, especially those that articulate form, in original and unique ways. This is, of course, generally recognized as one of the defining features of his style. My proposal would, however, enhance our appreciation of Bach's originality, for we would have to understand the relatively youthful composer of the English Suites, the Weimar organ chorales and preludes, and the Brandenburg Concertos as grappling with new and potentially powerful modulatory and articulatory techniques in genres that were not yet understood according to the sharply drawn formal structures and style categories delineated in modern textbooks. Bach nevertheless managed to create works that are both coherent and rich in their use of diverse compositional ideas. He did so within a context of adventurous compositional experimentation by numerous Italian and German contemporaries whose efforts led only gradually, and somewhat later than has been assumed, to the forms and genres that are now so confidently and comfortably recognized.

Appendix: Extracts from Johann Adolph Scheibe

CRITISCHER MUSIKUS (HAMBURG, 1745)

From "Das 69[.] Stück: Dienstags, den 22 December, 1739," on instrumental concertos (*Instrumentalconcerten*):

1. Aus der Beschreibung der Concerten, die ich anitzo gegeben habe, sieht man bereits, daß es dabey vornehmlich auf den Vorzug ankömmt, den man einem Instrumente, oder mehrern Instrumenten, insbesondere giebt, die nämlich die Hauptstimmen, oder die

---

101. The Fourth Brandenburg Concerto has also elicited debate as to whether it is "a solo concerto for violin with ripieno strings and woodwinds, or . . . a concerto grosso for a concertino of violin and woodwinds with ripieno strings," as Marissen puts it in *The Social and Religious Designs of J. S. Bach's Brandenburg Concertos* (Princeton, N.J.: Princeton University Press, 1995), 62. As Marissen suggests, this is a false dichotomy, although his argument that here Bach was "moving beyond the two-way (concertino/tutti) textural contrast of the traditional baroque concerto" (64) runs against the grain of what has been said here about Baroque "tradition" in such works.

concertirenden Stimmen spielen, und also das Wesen des Concerts eigentlich ausmachen. (631)

From the description of the concerto that I have previously given, one sees immediately that it depends chiefly on the predominance given to one or several instruments that play the main or solo parts and thus properly constitute the essence of the concerto.

2. Ein Concert, in welchem nur eine Concertstimme befindlich ist, wird aber folgendermaßen eingerichtet. Die Instrumente, welche der Concertstimme zur Begleitung zugegeben werden . . . gehen insgemein mit dem Hauptsatze des Concerts voraus, und die Concertstimme kann entweder inzwischen schweigen, oder auch mitspielen, nachdem es nämlich der Componist für gut hält. Das ist nun gleichsam das Rittornell. Nachdem dieses nun zu Ende: so tritt endlich die Concertstimme selbst ins besondere ein. Sie kann aber entweder mit dem wiederholten Hauptsatze, den das Rittornell zuvor gespielt hat, oder auch mit einem ganz neuen Satze anfangen. . . . Alle darinnen vorkommende Zwischensätze müssen neu, wohlausgesucht, klüglich angebracht und scharfsinnig verändert werden." (631–32)

A concerto in which only one solo part occurs will, however, be composed in the following manner. The instruments that are assigned to the accompaniment of the solo part . . . usually go first with the main passage of the concerto, and the solo part meanwhile can either be silent or play along, whichever the composer thinks best. This is, as it were, the ritornello. Once this has come to its conclusion, the solo part enters as such. It can begin either with a repetition of the main passage that the ritornello has previously played or with an entirely new passage. . . . All of the episodes found within must be new, well chosen, wisely employed, and ingeniously varied.

3. Endlich muß ich noch mit wenigem gedenken, daß man auch Concerten für ein Instrument allein verfertiget, ohne es durch andere begleiten zu lassen. Insonderheit machet man dergleichen Clavierconcerten oder Lautenconcerten. Bey dergleichen Stücken wird nun die Ordnung der Haupteinrichtung behalten, so wie sie in starken Concerten seyn soll. Der Baß und die Mittelstimme, die man hin und wieder der Ausfüllung wegen hinzuthut, müssen alsdann gleichsam die Nebenstimmen vorstellen. Und diejenigen Stellen, welche vor andern eigentlich das Wesen des Concerts ausmachen, müssen sich auf das deutlichste von den übrigen unterscheiden. Dieses kann auch dadurch mit sehr guter Art geschehen, wenn, nachdem der Hauptsatz eines geschwinden oder langsamen Satzes durch eine Cadenz geschlossen gewesen, besondere neue Sätze eintreten, und wenn diese wieder durch die Haupterfindung in veränderten Tonarten abgelöst werden. (637)

Finally I must consider briefly that one also prepares concertos for one solo instrument without accompaniment by others. Keyboard and lute concertos in particular are composed in this way. In such pieces one maintains the organization of the main plan such as occurs in fully scored concertos. The bass, as well as the middle parts that one introduces now and again to fill out [the harmony], must represent the accompanying parts, so to speak. And those places that above others properly constitute the essence of the concerto must be distinguished from the rest in the clearest manner. This can be accomplished in a good fashion if, after the main passage of a quick or slow movement has been concluded with a cadence, certain new passages enter, and if these alternate with the main theme in varying keys.

From "Das 74[.] Stück: Dienstags, den 20 Jenner [*sic*], 1740," on chamber sonatas:

4. Ich will aber zuvörderst von dreystimmigen und vierstimmigen Sonaten reden, davon die erstern insgemein *Trios*, die letztern aber *Quadros* genennet werden, hernach aber auch die übrigen etwas erläutern. Beyde Arten von Sonaten, von welchen ich zuerst reden will, werden eigentlich auf zweyerley Art eingerichtet, nämlich als eigentliche Sonaten, und dann auch auf Concertenart. (675)

I will first discuss three- and four-part sonatas, of which the former are generally called "trios," the latter "quartets"; then I will explain the others. The two types of sonatas that I will discuss first are properly composed in one of two ways, that is, as proper sonatas or as sonatas in the manner of a concerto.

5. Das so genannte Trio besteht aus drey besondern Stimmen, davon zwo die Oberstimmen sind, die dritte aber die Unterstimme oder den Baß dazu ausmachet. . . . Das eigentliche Wesen dieser Stücke aber ist überhaupt dieses, daß in allen Stimmen, vornehmlich aber in den Oberstimmen ein ordentlicher Gesang, und eine fugenmäßige Ausarbeitung seyn muß. Wenn sie nicht auf Concertenart eingerichtet werden: so darf man wenig kräuselnde und verändernde Sätze anbringen, sondern es muß durchaus eine bündige, fließende und natürliche Melodie vorhanden seyn. (676)

The so-called trio consists of three different parts, of which the first two comprise upper voices and the third a lower voice or bass. . . . The proper essence of these pieces is above all the presence of a regular melody in all parts, especially the upper voices, and a fugal working out. If it is not composed in the manner of a concerto, one may introduce slightly convoluted and variegated passages. But there must be a concise, flowing, and natural melody throughout.

6. Zuerst erscheint ein langsamer Satz, hierauf ein geschwinder oder lebhafter Satz; diesem folget ein langsamer, und zuletzt beschließt ein geschwinder und munterer Satz. Wiewohl man kann dann und wann den ersten langsamen Satz weglassen, und so fort mit dem lebhaften Satze anfangen. Dieses letztere pflegt man insonderheit zu thun, wenn man die Sonaten auf Concertenart ausarbeitet. (676–77)

First appears a slow movement, then a quick or lively movement; this is followed by a slow one and finally a quick, cheerful movement concludes [the sonata]. But now and then one can omit the first, slow movement and thus begin with the lively one. It is particularly customary to do this if one is composing a sonata in the manner of a concerto.

7. Der nunmehro folgende geschwinde oder lebhafte Satz wird insgemein auf Fugenart ausgearbeitet, wo er nicht selbst eine ordentliche Fuge ist. . . . Wenn das Trio concertenmäßig seyn soll: so kann auch ein Stimme stärker, als die andere, arbeiten, und also mancherley kräuselnde, laufende und verändernde Sätze hören lassen. Die Unterstimme kann auch in diesem Falle nicht so bündig, als in einer andern ordentlichen Sonate, gesetzet werden. (677–78)

The quick or lively movement that follows is usually worked out in the manner of a fugue, if it is not indeed a regular fugue. . . . If the trio is to be in concerto style, one [upper] part can work more fully than the other, and hence all sorts of convoluted, running, and variegated passages can be heard. The bass in this case can be composed less concisely than in another, regular sonata.

Sicilianos and Organ Recitals

Observations on J. S. Bach's Concertos

Christoph Wolff

The compositional history of Johann Sebastian Bach's concertos is one of the most important, interesting, challenging, and—as of late—hotly contested areas of Bach scholarship. What makes this subject particularly complicated is the proportionately large number of missing original sources.[1] Where the autograph sources have survived, they invariably represent fair copies of scores, working scores of later revisions, or performing parts—there is not a single instance where the composing score of a concerto in its first incarnation is extant. Hence, more often than not we lack hard evidence regarding when and how Bach composed a given concerto or which solo instrument he initially had in mind for it.

The chronology of the concertos has immediate implications for questions both of style and of form and, therefore, potentially wide ramifications regarding the overall integration of the concerto genre in Bach's instrumental and vocal oeuvre. Certainly the long-prevailing view that the bulk of Bach's instrumental works originated during the six-year period when the composer served as *Capellmeister* to the prince of Anhalt-Köthen has been replaced by a more differentiated picture[2] taking into consideration not only the fact that Bach's surviving instrumental output mirrors his lifelong activities as instrumentalist, but also research on the transmission of older secondary sources, their place of origin, and their scribes. Thus, a work like the G-Minor Fugue for Violin and Continuo (BWV 1026)[3] can clearly be linked to Bach's early Weimar years as chamber musician, and other such works can be dated to the 1730s, when for a decade Bach was director of the Leipzig Collegium Musicum, which held weekly performances.[4]

---

1. See Christoph Wolff, "Die Orchesterwerke J. S. Bachs:: Grundsätzliche Erwägungen zu Repertoire, Überlieferung und Chronologie," in BOW, 17–30.

2. See Christoph Wolff, "Bach's Leipzig Chamber Music," in *Bach: Essays on His Life and Music* (Cambridge, Mass.: Harvard University Press, 1991), 223–38.

3. See Klaus Hofmann, ed., NBA VII/8 (*Kammermusik*), KB, forthcoming.

4. See Christoph Wolff, *Johann Sebastian Bach: The Learned Musician* (New York: W. W. Norton, 2000), 351ff.

Still, significant lacunae remain. They pertain first of all to the unanswerable question as to the size of Bach's output of instrumental ensemble music. The work list in Bach's obituary offers little aid in this regard, for it identifies in the category of concerted chamber music only "various concertos for one, two, three, and four harpsichords" and then summarily mentions "a mass of other instrumental pieces of all sorts and for all kinds of instruments."[5] This imprecision also leaves open the question as to when Bach began composing instrumental ensemble music in general and concertos in particular. Curiously, we are much better informed about which pieces by other composers Bach knew and when he encountered them (e.g., sonatas by Legrenzi, Corelli, and Reinken in the years after 1700, or concertos by Vivaldi, Marcello, and Telemann after 1710) than about similar works he himself may have written at the time. Finally, they include a closer analysis of the stylistic interrelationship between Bach's output of instrumental ensemble music and that of his contemporaries[6] and that in his own vocal oeuvre.

In the Bach year 2000, Siegbert Rampe and Dominik Sackmann published a comprehensive survey of Bach's orchestral music. Their book devoted three chapters and nearly two hundred pages exclusively to Bach's concertos.[7] They recognized the need for a more reliable chronology of this repertoire, and by arriving at rather precise dates for all of Bach's concertos, they claimed to have established a definitive chronology for the eighteen extant works,[8] from the earliest to the latest versions. Most of the dates given by Rampe and Sackmann for the latest versions are not controversial, but their dating of the earliest versions advances a rather unique and unparalleled compositional history according to which all of Bach's concertos were composed between 1709 and 1720. Moreover, Rampe and Sackmann subdivide this time span of twelve years into distinct chronological segments, resulting in the timeline given in Table 1.[9]

5. NBR, 304.

6. The following studies have paved the way: Gregory G. Butler, "J. S. Bach's Reception of Tomaso Albinoni's Mature Concertos," *Bach Studies 2*, ed. Daniel R. Melamed (Cambridge: Cambridge University Press, 1995), 20–46; Steven Zohn and Ian Payne, "Bach, Telemann, and the Process of Transformative Imitation in BWV 1056/2 (156/1)," *Journal of Musicology* 17 (1999): 546–84; Steven Zohn, "Bach's Borrowings from Telemann," in *Telemann und Bach/Telemann-Beiträge* (*Magdeburger Telemann-Studien* 18), ed. Brit Reipsch and Wolf Hobohm (Hildesheim: Georg Olms Verlag, 2005), 111–19.

7. "Bach und das italienische Concerto," BOM, 65–79; "Bachs Konzerte: Die Entstehungsgeschichte ihrer Quellen," BOM, 80–176; and "Bachs Konzerte: Die Entstehungsgeschichte ihrer Musik," BOM, 177–249.

8. This count does not include arrangements such as the Concerto for Four Harpsichords (BWV 1065) (after Vivaldi) and multiple versions of one and the same music, such as the concertos BWV 1054, 1057, 1058, and 1062 based on concertos for other instruments.

9. Table 1 is an adaptation of the table in BOM, 242.

Table 1. Chronology of J. S. Bach's concertos proposed by Rampe and Sackmann

WEIMAR

1709–12
* First Brandenburg Concerto, early version (BWV 1046a)

1713
* The first and third movements of the Concerto for Two Harpsichords in C Major (BWV 1061a/1,3)

1714
* Two concerted movements for three violins in D minor later arranged as the first and third movements of the Concerto for Three Harpsichords, Strings, and Continuo (BWV 1063/1,3)
* Third Brandenburg Concerto (BWV 1048)

1714–15
* Violin concerto in D minor later arranged as the Concerto for Harpsichord, Strings, and Continuo (BWV 1052)

1715–17
* Concerto for Harpsichord, Flute, Violin, Strings, and Continuo in A Minor (BWV 1044/1,3)
* Second movement of the Concerto for Two Harpsichords in C Major (BWV 1061a/2)

KÖTHEN

1718
* Concerto for Violin, Strings, and Continuo in E Major (BWV 1042)
* Fifth Brandenburg Concerto, early version (BWV 1050a)
* Concerto for three violins in D major, later arranged as the Concerto for Three Harpsichords, Strings, and Continuo in C Major (BWV 1064)
* Concerto movement in D minor, later arranged as the fragmentary Concerto for Harpsichord, Strings, and Continuo in D Minor (BWV 1059)

1718–19
* Concerto for oboe d'amore in D major, later arranged as the Concerto for Harpsichord, Strings, and Continuo in E Major (BWV 1053)
* Concerto for oboe d'amore/viola d'amore in A major, later arranged as Concerto for Harpsichord, Strings, and Continuo in A Major (BWV 1055)

1719
* Trio sonata for two violins and continuo in D minor, later arranged as the Concerto for Two Violins, Strings, and Continuo (BWV 1043)
* Concerto for two violas in B♭ major, later arranged as the Sixth Brandenburg Concerto (BWV 1051)
* Concerted movement for violin in G minor, later arranged as the first movement of the Concerto for Harpsichord, Strings, and Continuo in F Minor (BWV 1056/1)
* Concerted movement for oboe in G minor, later arranged as the third movement of the Concerto for Harpsichord, Strings, and Continuo (BWV 1056/3)
* Concerted movement in F major, later arranged as the third movement of the First Brandenburg Concerto (BWV 1046/3)

Table 1. Continued

---

* Concerto for oboe and violin in C minor, later arranged as the Concerto for Two Harpsichord, Strings, and Continuo in C Minor (BWV 1060)

* Concerto for Violin, Strings, and Continuo in A Minor (BWV 1041)

1720

* Fifth Brandenburg Concerto (BWV 1050)

* Concerto for violin, two echo flutes, strings, and continuo, later arranged as the Fourth Brandenburg Concerto (BWV 1049)

* Concerto for trumpet, recorder, oboe, and violin, later arranged as the Second Brandenburg Concerto (BWV 1047)

According to Rampe and Sackmann, Bach's production of newly composed concertos ended in 1720. They state categorically that "his production of concertos had concluded by 1721."[10] Thus, in their scheme, the dedication score of the Brandenburg Concertos, dated March 24, 1721, marks a turning point, namely, the beginning of the process of revising, transcribing, and arranging earlier works, which then continues throughout the subsequent two decades. Finally, the score of the seven harpsichord concertos (BWV 1052–59) of 1738–39 denotes the absolute end of Bach's involvement with the concerto genre.

This sweeping chronological hypothesis, emphatically argued, suggests that Bach stopped composing new concertos before he had even reached the halfway point of the Köthen years. This in itself must be considered as questionable, for the concerto was the most popular genre of the time. (Whether or not Rampe and Sackmann are correct, on a purely statistical basis their view of Bach's concerto productivity from 1718 to 1720 resembles rather closely that of Johann Friedrich Fasch, who wrote well over fifty concertos during his tenure as *Cappellmeister* at the neighboring court of Anhalt-Zerbst.) But what could have induced Bach to stop composing concertos by the end of 1720? This is but one of the many questions raised by such a superficially grounded chronological scheme. Moreover, the lack of logic in the evolutionary trajectory of Bach's concerto style proposed by Rampe and Sackmann becomes evident when two pairs of examples are juxtaposed. They demonstrate the composer's evolving approach to the design of fast ritornellos on the one hand and slow melodic phrases on the other.

In the ritornellos of the opening movements of the Brandenburg Concertos, the bass line generally acts as subsidiary harmonic support for the predominant melody in the uppermost voice, which usually lends the movement its individual character. The

---

10. BOM, 241.

ritornello of the Second Brandenburg Concerto (BWV 1047)-which according to Rampe and Sackmann dates from 1720 and, along with the Fourth Brandenburg Concerto (BWV 1049), represents the final and most mature layer of Bach's concerto style—fits this pattern well, featuring a relatively static basso continuo line. (See Example 1.)

In comparison, the ritornello of the opening movement of the Concerto for Two Violins, Strings, and Continuo in D Minor (BWV 1043/1)—whose early version (supposedly a trio sonata) Rampe and Sackmann date at least one year earlier—features an explicitly contrapuntal bass line. The continuo part throughout is independent of the melody in the uppermost voice both melodically and rhythmically, thus diminishing its predominance. (See Example 2.)

Although the original score of BWV 1043 has not survived, a set of autograph parts from the period 1730–31 exists whose title, "*Concerto à 6*," clearly underlines the importance of the dynamic interplay of six parts. The viola part, rhythmically active and melodically conceived from the very first measures of the work, throws into question the hypothesis of a trio sonata prototype and suggests a date closer to 1730 than to 1720, let alone before 1720.

The structural design of slow movements raises serious questions, as well, if the middle movements of the Second and Fourth Brandenburg Concertos are taken to be representative of the most mature compositions of this kind. The Andante of the Fourth Brandenburg Concerto features a sequential pattern of short, mostly two-measure phrases. These phrases form pairs of corresponding members that exchange the prevailing melody between top and bottom voices. (See Example 3.)

Ex. 1. Allegro, Second Brandenburg Concerto (BWV 1047/1), mm. 1ff.

Ex. 2. Vivace, Concerto for Two Violins, Strings, and Continuo (BWV 1043/1), mm. 1ff.

Ex. 3. Andante, Fourth Brandenburg Concerto (BWV 1049/2), mm. 1ff.

The slow movement of the Second Brandenburg Concerto (BWV 1047/2) also is built on the principle of short phrases, whereas the slow middle movement of BWV 1043, supposedly composed much earlier, displays an extended lyrical melody in $\frac{12}{8}$ time shared among the two solo violins in alternating eighth- and sixteenth-note figuration. (See Example 4.)

There is no pre-Leipzig example for this kind of bel-canto melodic design. It finds its counterpart, though treated differently, in the "Aria" of the D-Major Ouverture (BWV 1068). Besides the obvious pastoral quality of this expansive $\frac{12}{8}$ movement, BWV 1043/2, with its wide-ranging and songlike melody in conjunct motion, finds no parallel among the Weimar and Köthen cantatas, not even among the Leipzig cantatas from the first annual cycle of 1723–24. However, from the middle of the second annual cycle, that is, beginning in the fall of 1724 and extending through the second half of the 1720s, there is a substantial number of arias in *"pastorale"* style, such as the opening movement of the cantata *Vergnügte Ruh, beliebte Seelenlust* (BWV 170), composed for the Sixth Sunday after Trinity in 1726 (28 July). (See Example 5.)

The *pastorale* arias[11] of the later Leipzig cantatas are complemented by a closely related aria type in "siciliano" style, usually in composite $\frac{6}{8}$ but also in $\frac{12}{8}$ meter. The two related types were widely disseminated across Europe in the second quarter of the eighteenth century, not only in opera arias, but also in other secular repertory, as well as in sacred music. Bach combines them in a stylish manner in the Sinfonia to the second part of the Christmas Oratorio (BWV 248/10), with its consistent and pointed dotted rhythm and irregularly accented, surprising harmonic shifts, the main distinguishing features of the siciliano style. Next to the pure siciliano type, perhaps the best-known example of the melancholic sort of "canzonetta siciliana" in Bach's work is the aria "Erbarme dich, Gott, um meiner Zähren willen" (BWV 244/39), from the

---

11. Extensive use of a pedal point to imitate the drone of bagpipes, obligatory in the strict pastorale type, is found among those arias that invoke genuine shepherd imagery, e.g., in the arias "Beglückte Herde, Jesu Schafe" (BWV 104/5) from the cantata *Du Hirte Israel, höre* (April 1724) and "Komm, leite mich" (BWV 175/2), from the cantata *Er rufet seinen Schafen mit Namen* (May 1725).

Ex. 4. Largo ma non tanto, Concerto for Two Violins, Strings, and Continuo
(BWV 1043/2), mm. 1ff.

Ex. 5. *Vergnügte Ruh, beliebte Seelenlust* (BWV 170/1), mm. 1ff.

St. Matthew Passion of 1727. But also the earlier aria "Bleibt, ihr Engel, bleibt bei mir" from the Michelmas cantata *Es erhub sich ein Streit* (BWV 19) of 1726, with its emphatic and edgy dotted melody, exemplifies a particularly expressive siciliano underscoring the text, "daß mein Fuß nicht möge gleiten" (that my foot may not stumble). (See Example 6.)

The same year, three weeks after St. Michael's Day on the Eighteenth Sunday after Trinity (October 20), Bach performed the cantata *Gott soll allein mein Herze haben* (BWV 169). Its fifth movement, the E-minor aria "Stirb in mir, Welt," represents an equally expressive vintage siciliano and, besides manifesting its clear typological identification with BWV 19/5, shows a particularly close musical resemblance to the earlier work. However, unlike BWV 19/5, the aria BWV 169/5 was not newly composed just before its first performance. The aria for alto, obbligato organ, and orchestra was borrowed along with the sinfonia to the same cantata for obbligato organ and orchestra from preexisting concerted movements that Bach reworked in the late 1730s as the Concerto for Harpsichord, Strings, and Continuo in E Major (BWV 1053). (See Example 7.)

The example from BWV 169/5 demonstrates the elemental identity of vocal and instrumental realizations of the siciliano style and thereby the immediate correlations between the two movement types—aria and slow concerto movement.

The siciliano movement BWV 1053/2 is by no means an isolated example, for several

Ex. 6. "Bleibt, ihr Engel, bleibt bei mir" (BWV 19/5), mm. 1ff.

Ex. 7. "Stirb in mir, Welt und alle deine Liebe" (BWV 169/5), mm. 1ff.

of Bach's instrumental concertos include middle movements that feature exactly the same kind of siciliano/pastorale style, either in slow $\frac{12}{8}$ or $\frac{6}{8}$ meter. Altogether, six out of a total of eighteen concertos contain such movements, two of them specifically headed "*Siciliano*" and "*Alla Siciliana*," respectively:

$\frac{6}{8}$

BWV 1063/2: *Alla Siciliana* (F major)
BWV 1061/2: *Adagio* (A minor)

$\frac{12}{8}$

BWV 1053/2: *Siciliano* (C♯ minor)
BWV 1043/2: *Largo ma non tanto* (F major)
BWV 1055/2: *Larghetto* (F♯ minor)
BWV 1060/2: *Largo ovvero Adagio* (E♭ major)

Given the palpable typological parallels between concerto movements and cantata arias (as exemplified by BWV 169/5 but present in many similar arias)[12] composed after 1724 on the one hand, and on the other, the complete lack of such parallels prior to 1724, the question arises as to whether these concerto movements could indeed have been composed prior to the Leipzig period as Rampe and Sackmann claim.

The present inquiry approaches the concerto repertoire by drawing attention to a

---

12. For example, "Ich will leiden, ich will schweigen" (BWV 87/6) from the cantata *Bisher habt ihr nichts gebeten* (May 1725).

particular movement type that may shed light on the stylistic context from which these works arose. However, rather than drawing broad conclusions for all six concertos, I propose to focus on the E-Major Concerto (BWV 1053) and the murky compositional history not only of its Siciliano movement, but of its outer movements, as well, and, in addition, the much-contested identity of its original solo instrument.

BWV 1053, along with its extant and supposed models, offers a special case in point and one with considerable ramifications for the thesis proposing Leipzig origins for this concerto. Its primary source is the autograph composing score of BWV 1052–59, P 234, written out by Bach around 1738. The keyboard solo parts in the score show numerous traces of heavy revision. Earlier versions of BWV 1053/1 and BWV 1053/2 are to be found in the "Sinfonia" and the aria "Stirb in mir, Welt" (BWV 49/1,5) from the cantata *Gott soll allein mein Herze haben* (BWV 169) and of BWV 1053/3 in the "Sinfonia," from the cantata *Ich geh und suche mit Verlangen* (BWV 49/1).

The relationship of BWV 169/5 and BWV 1053/2 has already been discussed, including the fact that the former is not an original vocal composition but a concerto arrangement. Conceptually, however, this aria-concerto movement conveys much closer connections with other cantata arias, not only in its strict ritornello structure, but also in its affect and certain of its declamatory and textual details. It resembles closely the E-minor aria "Ach, schläfrige Seele" (adagio, $\frac{3}{8}$) from the cantata *Mache dich, mein Herz, bereit* (BWV 115/2), composed for the Twenty-second Sunday after Trinity in 1724 (5 November). (See Example 8.)

The other question concerns the solo instrument in the original concerted movements that served as *Vorlage* for both BWV 169/1,5 and BWV 49/1, and for BWV 1053/1–3. For three of the seven harpsichord concertos—BWV 1054, 1057, and 1058—the original concerto version has been preserved, and in all three the solo part was conceived originally for violin. This fact prompted Wilhelm Rust, editor of the concertos in the BG edition, to assume that solo violin parts for the most part served as models for the solo parts in all seven concertos, especially for the D-minor concerto.[13] Later Bach scholars, however, no longer uniformly share Rust's opinion, especially not in the case of the E-major, A-major, and F-minor concertos.[14]

Werner Breig, editor of these concertos for the NBA, left open the question of the original solo instrument of BWV 1053, stating cautiously that the lost first version of the concerto was written "for a concertato melody instrument" and adding that "the question concerning its solo instrument and key has not found a universally accepted answer."[15] Despite the questions surrounding the identity of the original solo instru-

13. BG 17, XIV.

14. See KBT.

15. See Werner Breig, ed., NBA VII/4 (*Konzerte für Cembalo*), KB, 86–88.

Ex. 8. "Ach schläfrige Seele, wie ruhest du noch" (BWV 115/2), mm. 1ff.

ment, there are several modern reconstructions of this concerto in circulation with the solo part played variously by oboe (in F or E♭ major), oboe d'amore (in D major), and viola (in E♭ major).[16]

Breig's prudently cautious approach to the questions of the original solo instrument and original key is well founded, for none of the reconstructions referred to here is without its problems. The solo viola arrangement calls for downward octave transposition, a process nowhere else required in a Bach concerto. The oboe and oboe d'amore ascriptions are problematic, as well, because none of the keys, D, E♭, or F major, is truly idiomatic to the instruments. As well, the endless chains of sixteenth notes in BWV 1053/3 offer no room for normal breathing technique. The movement can, therefore, be played only by applying circular breathing or by leaving out a note here and there.

However, there is a fairly logical alternative if one allows for the possibility that the original instrument may not have been a "melody instrument" and, at the same time, if one takes into consideration a known Bach document that has never been subjected to a close reading.[17] A newspaper report of 21 September 1724 describes two recitals given by Bach on the new Silbermann organ in St. Sophia's Church[18] in Dresden:

> *Dresden, 21 September 1725.* When the Capell-Director from Leipzig, Mr. Bach, came here recently, he was very well received by the local virtuosos at the court and in

16. See NBA VII/4; KB, 87f.

17. The following discussion presents an expansion of a statement regarding the implications of this document made in Christoph Wolff, *Johann Sebastian Bach*, 318n4. (The version in F major for solo transverse flute proposed as an alternative by Siegele [KBT, 142] has not been published.)

18. The organ (Hauptwerk, Oberwerk, Pedal: 30 stops) was completed by Gottfried Silbermann in 1720 (see note 31). Bach gave at least one other recital there on September 14, 1731—again "in the presence of all the court musicians and virtuosos" (NBR, 311), yet no reference is made to the music he played on this occasion. Subsequently, his son Wilhelm Friedemann served as organist at St. Sophia's from 1733 to 1746. Both the church and its organ were completely destroyed in the Allied bombing of 1945.

the city since he is greatly admired by all of them for his musical adroitness and art. Yesterday and the day before, in the presence of the same, he performed for over an hour on the new organ in St. Sophia's Church preludes and various concertos, with intervening soft instrumental music (*diversen Concerten mit unterlauffender Doucen Instrumental-Music*) in all keys.[19]

The specific reference to "diverse concertos with intervening [supporting, accompanying] soft instrumental music" can refer only to concertos for solo organ with string accompaniment.[20] The accompanying ensemble was most likely provided by the Dresden court musicians led by Johann Georg Pisendel, whom Bach had known for about twenty years and who in 1717 had arranged the competition between Bach and Louis Marchand. The phrase "in all keys" must not be taken literally, for playing preludes and concertos in all twenty-four keys could hardly be accomplished in two recitals, even when each lasted "over an hour." The reference does suggest, however, that Bach played in many different keys, including some remote ones, in order to demonstrate what the new instrument was capable of.

Which "diverse concerte" could Bach have played in Dresden on September 19 and 20, 1725? No concertos for solo organ and strings by Bach are transmitted. The only compositions of this kind occur in the series of cantatas featuring obbligato organ from the third annual cycle (1725–27), BWV 35, 49, 146, 169, and 188. The cantatas incorporate concerto movements, but never more than two from the same concerto. However, four of them include all six movements from the later D-Minor and E-Major Concertos (BWV 1052 and 1053), curiously, the first two concertos entered in P 234. This raises the possibility that Bach opened the collection with concertos that, from the outset, were conceived with the keyboard as solo instrument. BWV 1052 and 1053 definitely existed in some form by 1726, and if indeed their original versions were keyboard concertos, both would be natural candidates for the Dresden recital programs of September 1725.

The origin of P 234 more than a decade later does not undermine this supposition, for it leaves open the possibility that Bach developed the concept of the harpsichord concerto only in the 1730s.[21] Nor do the cantatas with obbligato organ suggest that the combination of organ and orchestra in the form of concerto movements was invented solely for this purpose. Unfortunately, the surviving sources do not allow us to

19. NBR, 117.

20. Of all contemporaneous references to Bach's recitals, this is the only one that hints at the kinds of pieces he played.

21. The late emergence of the idea of a concerto for harpsichord and orchestra is proposed by Werner Breig, "Johann Sebastian Bach und die Entstehung des Klavierkonzerts," *Archiv für Musikwissenschaft* 36 (1979): 21–48.

Plate 1. Dresden, St. Sophia's Church: Final Design of Organ Facade (Gottfried Silbermann, George Bähr, c. 1719). Reproduced by permission of Staatliche Kunstsammlungen Dresden-Kupferstichkabinett.

track the origins of the keyboard concerto in Bach's oeuvre beyond the special—and different—use of the harpsichord in the Fifth Brandenburg Concerto (BWV 1050)[22] or beyond the Weimar arrangements of orchestral concertos by Vivaldi and others for solo organ (BWV 592–96) and solo harpsichord (BWV 972–87) from around 1713–14. Nevertheless, the supposition seems logical that Bach experimented with and composed concertos for keyboard with orchestral accompaniment as court organist in Weimar, where the duke, as the composer's obituary put it, "fired him with the desire to try every possible artistry in his treatment of the organ."[23] Hence, one can hardly go wrong in placing Bach's initial experimentation with the keyboard concerto sometime between his arrangements of Italian concertos for solo keyboard and the composition of the original D-major version for three violins of the Concerto for Three Harpsichords, Strings, and Continuo in C Major (BWV 1064), in other words, sometime during the second half of his Weimar period.

This may have direct implications for the genesis of the D-Minor Concerto (BWV 1052) and its original solo instrument. Apart from the view now rejected by most Bach scholars that the model for BWV 1052 was the work of another composer, the opinion first advanced in 1869 by Wilhelm Rust,[24] that the work began its life as a violin concerto, is that which prevails today. Werner Breig,[25] in particular, has argued forcefully that this putative D-minor violin concerto originated in Weimar sometime after 1714,[26] primarily because of the approach to ritornello form, a certain stylistic incoherence, and aspects of compositional technique that differ from most of Bach's other concertos. However, although the arguments in favor of a Weimar dating after 1714 are most convincing, the traditional view that BWV 1052 was conceived as a violin concerto must be questioned. The case actually requires a detailed separate study, but the following principal points can be advanced.

The typical violin figuration (bariolage, etc.) and virtuosic passagework in BWV 1052

---

22. The dedication score of the Brandenburgs dates from the spring of 1721 and does not indicate when BWV 1050 was composed. Yet the earlier version BWV 1050a and the two surviving solo cadenzas for the harpsichord part suggest a performance history that goes back perhaps to the late Weimar period. Pieter Dirksen, "The Background to Bach's Fifth Brandenburg Concerto," *Proceedings of the International Harpsichord Symposium Utrecht 1990* (Utrecht, 1992), 157–85, presents a plausible argument for a performance of the concerto in conjunction with Bach's Dresden visit in the fall of 1717. Christoph Wolff and Martin Zepf, *Die Orgeln Johann Sebastian Bachs.: Ein Handbuch* (Leipzig: Evangelische Verlagsanstalt, 2006), 35–37.

23. NBR, 300.

24. See BG 17, xiii–xv. For a summary of the various viewpoints, see NBA VII/4, KB, 52.

25. "Bach's Violinkonzert d-Moll—Studien zu seiner Gestalt und Entstehungsgeschichte," BJ 62 (1976): 7–34.

26. A view basically shared, if concretized, by Rampe and Sackmann.

that Wilhelm Rust drew attention to are nowhere to be found in so extreme a form in the A-Minor and E-Major Concertos for Violin (BWV 1041, 1042) or in any other solo violin piece by Bach. There is no question that the general concept of the Italian solo concerto, particularly the design of its virtuosic solo part, was shaped significantly by violin technique. As the genre of the solo concerto was so closely identified with the violin concerto, it would not be at all surprising for Bach, himself a violin and keyboard player, to employ idiomatic violin figuration in the absence of equivalent keyboard models for the development of virtuosic keyboard passagework in his concertos for keyboard solo—a practice that had its parallel in an earlier seventeenth-century keyboard practice, the "imitatio violistica."[27] Bach's transcriptions of Vivaldi's opus 3 display direct translations of characteristic violin figuration into idiomatic passagework for the keyboard.[28] The many traces of corrections in the harpsichord solo parts of P 234 may not, therefore, reflect the process of transcribing violin parts into harpsichord parts. They could just as well, perhaps even better, be reinterpreted as a working out of further refinements, improvements, and amplifications to the older "violin style" keyboard figuration.

Another question pertains to the more specific elaboration of the continuo-related left-hand harpsichord parts in P 234. Early keyboard concertos, whether by Bach, Handel, or other composers, all have in common a clear emphasis on the right-hand part and the treble register. The left-hand parts in the related cantata movements for obbligato organ are by and large identical with the basso continuo parts. However, the apparent emphasis on the right-hand parts may not point to derivation from a supposed solo part for violin, oboe, or other melody instrument but may rather reflect specific performance conditions. If—as the evidence suggests—the solo organ parts in these movements were indeed played by the composer,[29] he would not have needed a detailed realization of the left-hand part.[30] Bass and treble lines would have been sufficient in defining the scaffolding for the soloist's improvisatory elaboration. Moreover, the registrational requirements for the obbligato organ were different from those for ordinary continuo accompaniment. In order to achieve a balance between the organ

27. See Christoph Wolff, "Buxtehudes freie Orgelmusik und die Idee der 'imitatio violistica,'" in *Dietrich Buxtehude und die europäische Musik seiner Zeit. Bericht über das Lübecker Symposion 1987*, ed. Arnfried Edler and Friedhelm Krummacher. *Kieler Schriften zur Musikwissenschaft* 35 (Kassel: Bärenreiter, 1990): 310–19.

28. See, for example, the organ transcription of Vivaldi's A-minor concerto in BWV 593/3, m. 75ff.

29. See Laurence Dreyfus, "The metaphorical soloist," *Early Music* 13 (1985): 247.

30. All cantatas with obbligato organ lack a separate organ part, an unusual phenomenon in the transmission of the performance parts for Bach's Leipzig cantatas. This suggests that the composer played the solo part from the score and left the conducting in all likelihood to the chief choir prefect.

and the orchestral ensemble of winds and strings, the use of plenum-style registration in the Rückpositiv of the organs at St. Nicholas's and St. Thomas's was necessary. The fact that these organs were not tuned in equal temperament would have placed limitations on chordal playing, so that emphasis on the treble part was a given.

That the Leipzig cantatas with obbligato organ were performed in large churches with two thousand or more worshippers present may help us to understand yet another phenomenon—the varying effectiveness of the available keyboard instruments used for different purposes. As for keyboard concertos with orchestral accompaniment, the organ was far more successful for public presentations, whereas the harpsichord was better suited to the more intimate setting of private performances. In this light, Bach's choice of the organ loft of St. Sophia's Church as a venue for the public concerts with the Dresden court Capelle was most appropriate.

Although any discussion of the program for the 1725 Dresden recitals remains entirely speculative, early versions of BWV 1052 and 1053 for organ solo are plausible given the chronological proximity of the related cantatas and the lack of any other candidates. Of the two works, the D-Minor Concerto (BWV 1052), although it represented an older piece, on account of its unparalleled virtuosity had not lost its special appeal as a daring showpiece. Even later, around 1738, it was still deemed so exemplary and attractive by Bach that he chose it to head the collection of concertos in P 234. In contrast, BWV 1053, as a recent composition, would have represented the modern counterpart to the earlier composition, its Siciliano movement exemplifying an advanced harmonic language of novel expressivity.

In addition, the earlier version of BWV 1053 for organ solo would have been the perfect match for the Silbermann organ at St. Sophia's, an instrument different from the ones available to Bach in Leipzig.[31] The keys of the movements of this concerto correspond nicely with the report about Bach's playing "in all keys," for the keys of E major and C♯ minor, with their signatures of four sharps, were at the extreme end of the spectrum normally present in compositions of the time. In fact, an E-major concerto for organ solo would help solve the many problems that have long plagued scholars, including the question of the original key of the concerto:

1. The key of E major (not E♭ or D major) would explain the frequent copying errors (entry of notes originally a second too high) in the ripieno parts (notated in D major) of the autograph score of BWV 169/1.

2. The temperament of the organ of St. Sophia's would have facilitated playing in all keys. The instrument (tuned in *Cammerton*) featured the unusual manual

---

31. Ulrich Dähnert, *Historische Orgeln in Sachsen* (Leipzig: Deutscher Verlag für Musik, 1980), 84f.; Frank-Harald Groß, *Die Orgeln Gottfried Silbermanns* (Dresden: Michel Sandstein Verlag, 2001), 141–43.

compass C, D–d''' and thus accommodated the highest note in ʙᴡᴠ 1053/1, C♯'''. (Bach's Leipzig organs [tuned in *Chorton*] had the normal manual compass, C, D–c'''.)

3. In cantata ʙᴡᴠ 169/1, Bach had to transpose the first two movements a whole tone down from E major and C♯ minor for two reasons—first, to accommodate the *Chorton* tuning of the organ a whole step above the *Cammerton* tuning of the other instruments, and second, to make available the tone c♯''' (b" *Chorton*) on the Leipzig organs, which extended up only to C'''. To make this possible, he transposed the autograph score of the cantata movement down a whole tone to D (*Cammerton*), with the obbligato organ part in C major (*Chorton*), thus lowering the highest note to b".

4. The third movement of the concerto required no downward transposition, as the highest note in the solo part of the "Sinfonia" ʙᴡᴠ 49/1 is b".

5. The melodic figuration and passagework in the E-major and C♯-minor concerto movements are entirely consistent with idiomatic keyboard writing. Neither key presents difficulties, nor do breathing problems exist. The left-hand part required no elaboration, for it would have been improvised by the composer. The extensive revisions made to the solo part subsequently in ᴘ 234 may well reflect Bach's improvisatorial practice in treating the left-hand part and not necessarily a conceptually new approach.

The chronological problems also disappear if this proposed original E-major organ concerto is seen in the context of the siciliano arias of the second and third Leipzig cantata cycles, which appear for the first time in the fall of 1724. The analytical observations made by Butler,[32] who has shown how ʙᴡᴠ 1053/3 adopted certain formal and stylistic features from the innovative *Concerti a cinque*, op. 9, by Tomaso Albinoni (Amsterdam, 1722), support a likely date of composition for this concerto in the mid-1720s.

As we possess no musical sources for the two hypothetical "Dresden" organ concertos, there remains the question of the actual musical text of both the solo and orchestral parts. The four cantata scores[33] incorporating the six concerto movements indicate that the instrumental settings were integrated without substantive compositional changes. The orchestral scoring was augmented for performance in Leipzig by the addition of woodwinds to the original strings-only accompaniment: two regular hautbois plus taille in ʙᴡᴠ 146/1 and 188/1 (compare with ʙᴡᴠ 1052/1,3); and two hautbois d'amour

32. "J. S. Bach's reception of Tomaso Albinoni's mature concertos" (see note 6).

33. ʙᴡᴠ 146: Am. B. 538 = score copied by Johann Friedrich Agricola (ʙᴡᴠ 1052/1,2); ʙᴡᴠ 188: scattered fols. (see BC A 154) = incomplete autograph score, cf. BC A 154 (ʙᴡᴠ 1052/3); ʙᴡᴠ 169: ᴘ 93 = autograph score (ʙᴡᴠ 1053/1,2); ʙᴡᴠ 49: ᴘ 111 = autograph score (ʙᴡᴠ 1053/3).

and taille in BWV 169/1 and one hautbois d'amour in BWV 49/1 (compare with BWV 1053/1,3). The keyboard solo parts required few if any adjustments.[34]

In the case of BWV 1052 we possess additional evidence—a set of performing parts copied after 1734 by Carl Philipp Emanuel Bach, St 350. This source was long considered to be an early version of the D-Minor Concerto (BWV 1052a)[35] until Georg von Dadelsen claimed it to be an independent arrangement by the copyist[36]—a view accepted by the NBA, which published it as the work of C. P. E. Bach.[37] There is, however, neither source nor musical evidence establishing the younger Bach as arranger. Rather, all indications are that BWV 1052a, as part of his father's *Nachlass*, had served the Bach son as repertoire for performances with his Collegium Musicum at Frankfurt an der Oder between 1734 and 1738.[38] The string parts of BWV 1052a represent the earliest extant layer in the traceable history of the work, apparently pointing to a stage of the keyboard concerto that precedes the cantata adaptations of 1726, whereas the solo part may incorporate some later revisions by the composer independent of and preceding his work on P 234.

Finally, this raises the question: For what purpose did Bach gather together the seven harpsichord concertos BWV 1052–59 in P 234? Regardless of what Bach performed in 1725 in Dresden, the D-minor and E-major concertos that open the collection clearly had an extended performance history that in all probability began in the Weimar and early Leipzig years, respectively. At any rate, both concertos—their solos played either by organ or cembalo, depending on occasion and space—could hardly have emerged as keyboard concertos only in the mid- or late 1730s. However, if P 234 does not, as traditionally assumed, represent the very document that embodies the birth of the "Bach harpsichord concerto" but instead marks the endpoint of a rather lengthy involvement of the composer-virtuoso with the genre of the keyboard concerto, what was his intent when he compiled the collection and in the process put the finishing touches on this repertoire around 1738?

---

34. In the autograph score, the obbligato organ parts are notated at the lower octave in the soprano clef along with the specification of 4' registration in order for the parts to fit the manual compass of the Leipzig organs.

35. Rust, BG 17. For a clarification, see Wolff, "Die Orchesterwerke," 21n15.

36. See Georg von Dadelsen, *Bemerkungen zur Handschrift Johann Sebastian Bachs, seiner Familie und seines Kreises. Tübingen Bach Studien herausgegeben von Walter Gerstenberg*, 1 (Trossingen, 1957), 40.

37. NBA VII/4, KB, 317–67.

38. See Peter Wollny, "Zur Überlieferung der Instrumentalwerke Johann Sebastian Bachs: Der Quellenbesitz Carl Philipp Emanuel Bachs," BJ 82 (1996): 7–21. Wollny (p. 9) dates St 355 after 1734 and before 1740.

Again, there is no definitive answer either to this question or to that as to why Bach broke off work on the score, leaving the D-Minor Concerto (BWV 1059) as a fragment.[39] The revisions of other works, such as the so-called Eighteen Chorales and the compilation of the Well-Tempered Clavier II, also datable to ca. 1738, suggest that Bach was taking stock of his most important creations for the keyboard in all major genres, reviewing, revising, preserving the materials, and considering much of it for publication. The continuing Clavier-Übung series and other publication projects Bach undertook in the 1740s certainly raise the possibility that Bach had publication of the collection in mind. That publishing keyboard concertos was by no means a hopeless task at the time is demonstrated by the fact that C. P. E. Bach published his first concerto in 1745—curiously enough, engraved, printed, and published by his father's publisher, Balthasar Schmid of Nuremberg.[40]

39. For a tentative explanation, see Werner Breig, "Bachs Cembalokonzert-Fragment in d-Moll (BWV 1059)," BJ 65 (1979): 29–36.

40. Postscript: Gregory Butler's essay elsewhere in this volume came to my attention only after the completion of this paper. Our conclusions are in general agreement regarding 1723–26 as the period during which the original version of the later E-Major Concerto (BWV 1053) was prepared. However, Butler argues that all three movements originated independently of one other and were brought together either shortly before or after they were arranged for BWV 169 and 49, whereas I see no compelling reason for heterogeneous origins of the three concerto movements. In this regard, I would stress the striking similarity between BWV 1052 and 1053, where, in both cases, the first and second movements appear in one cantata and the third appears in another, in the case of BWV 169 and BWV 49, written just two weeks later.

CONTRIBUTORS

GREGORY BUTLER is senior professor of music at the School of Music, University of British Columbia in Vancouver, British Columbia. He is the author of *J. S. Bach's Clavier-Übung III: The Making of a Print* and numerous articles on the first editions of Bach's works. He has also written extensively on Bach's concertos and is presently researching the composer's Leipzig organ works. He was elected president of the American Bach Society in 2004.

PIETER DIRKSEN is a noted musicologist, harpsichordist, and organist and has published widely on keyboard music of Sweelinck and Scheidemann. He is the author of a monograph on Bach's *Kunst der Fuge*, and his scholarly interest in J. S. Bach has centered on the keyboard works and the concertos.

DAVID SCHULENBERG is author of *The Keyboard Music of J. S. Bach* and *Music of the Baroque*. He performs and records on harpsichord, fortepiano, and other historical keyboard instruments and is editing volumes of keyboard sonatas and concertos for *Carl Philipp Emanuel Bach: The Complete Works*. Since 2001, he has been professor and chair of the Department of Music at Wagner College in New York City.

CHRISTOPH WOLFF is Adams University Professor, Harvard University. He has published widely on all aspects of Bach's music. He is editor of the *New Bach Reader* (1998), and his Bach biography, *Johann Sebastian Bach: The Learned Musician* (2000) was a finalist for a Pulitzer Prize. He has been director of the Bach-Archiv, Leipzig, since 2001.

GENERAL INDEX

INDEX OF BACH'S COMPOSITIONS

The University of Illinois Press
is a founding member of the
Association of American University Presses.

Composed in 10/14 Janson Text
by Jim Proefrock
at the University of Illinois Press
Designed by Dika Eckersley
Manufactured by Sheridan Books, Inc.

University of Illinois Press
1325 South Oak Street
Champaign, IL 61820-6903
www.press.uillinois.edu